Untimely Love

By
Dawn Brotherton

Blue Dragon Publishing

Untimely Love

Published by Blue Dragon Publishing, LLC

Williamsburg, VA

www.Blue-Dragon-Publishing.com

ISBN 978-1-939696-53-3

ISBN 978-1-939696-55-7 (ePub)

Library of Congress Control Number: 2019950241

FIC02702 FICTION / Romance / Contemporary

Cover by Resa Reid

To my muse who gave me the writing bug.

Chapter 1

She was trapped.

Her boss entered the room and leaned against the richly paneled wall with his arms folded across his chest. The smirk on his face spoke volumes.

Watching him out of the corner of her eye, she went about her business, all the while careful to keep the heavy wooden table between herself and her pursuer.

"Have you thought about my proposal?" he asked with an almost perceptible purr in his voice.

She glanced up, then went back to sorting and stacking the papers spread across the tabletop in front of her. She was determined to finish quickly so she could leave without an incident. "I don't remember you giving me a choice in the matter," she said without meeting his eye.

"There are always options."

The young lady finished her last stack and began putting the papers into presentation folders. "I don't like what you consider options."

"Ah, come on, a promotion is not something to be taken lightly," he protested as he made a show of straightening a painting that had moved out of alignment.

She paused in her work and looked at him. "You mean the promotion I'd get if I would agree to a weekend getaway in Atlanta?"

"What a great deal! I even offered to pay."

She turned her head away from him and stared out the large windows overlooking the city. The glass was tinted to keep out the heat, so it was hard to tell if it was dark outside or only appeared to be. She thought about her next words carefully.

"So, you think moving into a corner office in exchange for meeting you for a nooner at the Belmont Suite is a good deal?"

"For both of us, I'm sure," he said, causing her to shudder in disgust.

She pulled a cardboard box from under the table and began loading the blue folders into it.

"I don't know why you're acting so cold. I can make things happen for you in this company." He feigned concern. "I'm only looking out for your best interests."

She ignored his lewd gaze that undressed her. "And what was the third option? Oh, I remember. I could write my own ticket to the top of this corporation simply by being at your beck and call when your wife just wouldn't do. Is that about right?" She folded her arms across her chest, mocking his initial pose.

"You make it sound like such a punishment. We all play the game. I'm glad you're getting the hang of it." His smirk widened into a wolfish grin. The man cleaned up nicely in an expensive suit, but it couldn't hide the filth within. "It has worked for others, and I haven't heard any complaints."

The young woman made no comment as she weighed her decision. He took her silence as assent. "My girl in the front office will make the reservations. I'll let you pick the hotel. Hell, I'll even take you out for a romantic dinner." He pushed away from the wall and took a step toward her.

She came out from behind the oak table she had been using as her barricade and put her hand in the center of his chest, stopping him in his tracks. Then she stepped around him to the door. "Let me tell you what's going to happen," she began, turning to face him.

His sly smile grew into a devilish grin.

She continued, "First, you're going to get your sorry excuse for manhood away from me and keep it that way. I'm no more interested than your wife is." A look of confusion covered his face.

"Second, you're going to sign my request for promotion because I'm the most qualified." Now his face turned red with indignation, and he started to protest.

She stopped him cold with her next statement. "Third, you can turn in your resignation," she said, opening the door to the next room with a flourish to reveal a very angry human resource specialist. From the look on his face, it was evident he had overheard their whole conversation.

"And," she finished with scorn, "have your girl make your reservations in Hell."

From the seats gathered around the stage, the crowd applauded. The heroine and villain joined hands and gave an exaggerated bow.

Jamie Woods clapped too as she joined the actors in the center of the room. She shook hands with them, and they took their seats, with much back slapping and wolf whistles.

Jamie faced the audience. "What I want you to take away from this is there is always a way out. No one has to put up with sexual harassment. If you find yourself in an uncomfortable situation, let us help you."

Jamie paced at the front of the room, the stage prop furniture behind her. Hundreds of eyes followed her, some more interested than others, but she did have their attention. In this fading economy, any ideas to make the company stronger meant more assurance their jobs were safe.

The thirty-three-year-old executive was comfortable speaking in front of others and looked natural in charge. As she spoke, Jamie unconsciously brushed chestnut hair away from her face. She moved easily in front of the audience; her long legs covered by linen pants ending in sensible, flat shoes. At 5'8", Jamie didn't need the extra height and had always been more interested in comfort than fashion. Her sapphire blue blouse was tucked in, showing off her shapely figure. She liked wearing blue. An old flame had once told her it brought out the azure crystals in her eyes. Using the cheesy line didn't gain him any brownie points.

"While we have a captured audience, Steve said I could take a few moments to introduce a new campaign we will be implementing. Growth within Winkler and Stein Solar is good for all of us," Jamie explained. "And you can be part of the recruiting effort by helping me get the word out."

The audience was in rapt attention as she began to outline her ideas for taking Winkler and Stein Solar into the next century through innovative recruiting to help attract the experts they would need to add a new division to the company. She was the head of the human resources department, but she knew a good marketing strategy was crucial for the success of her plan. Her division chiefs had pitched her ideas to various people within the marketing department, and they helped her solidify her plan. The last stop before making the final proposal to the boss was a wrap-up meeting with the marketing director. So far, their contact had been brief, but he seemed supportive.

While she spoke, Jamie strained to hold her temper as the asshole in the front row attempted to make an impression on someone. Leaning back in his seat with his arms crossed in front of him and legs outstretched, he peppered Jamie with questions and comments that had no place in this forum.

After his fourth interruption, Jamie approached him with a laser pointer extended in an offering. "Kevin's going to take over this lecture. He's apparently the expert."

A chuckle rippled through the audience but stopped when Jamie took a seat and pulled out her cell phone, feigning disinterest, and pretending to text someone. People whispered to each other, wondering if this was planned. Kevin was dumbfounded, still holding the laser pointer Jamie had given him.

"Come on, Kevin," a co-worker from the back of the room goaded. "Tell us how you would do it." The crowd laughed again, breaking the tension.

Kevin mumbled an apology to Jamie and handed her back the laser pointer.

"Wise choice," Kevin's boss said, and the crowd snickered.

Jamie stood and began again. She was enthusiastic about her topic and knew her ground-breaking ideas should attract the best and brightest from the colleges and even other industries. She was on a roll and nearing the end of her presentation when she looked over the audience and saw the marketing director staring at her. She could tell from the grin on his face he wasn't listening. She was frustrated at not being taken seriously; she was ready to explode—especially because marketing was so important to her plan. She took a deep breath to regain control.

"Mr. Simons, what would you suggest in this situation?"

Heads turned to focus on Ben. He was startled and caught off guard. He had been daydreaming and had no idea what the topic was. His face flushed. He tried to recover but was in no position to do so. Jamie waited patiently.

"Ah, Ms. Woods, you have succeeded in stumping the chump," he said lamely. "We'll have to collaborate more on this topic."

Having made her point, Jamie turned back to her presentation and wrapped it up. It was only a small victory but was gratifying after their uncomfortable first meeting.

Chapter 2

The first time Jamie had encountered Ben was at a company picnic. It was a beautiful summer day, and she was enjoying the shade of a large oak tree. The sky was mostly clear with only a few random puffy clouds to throw shadows over the park when they passed in front of the sun.

Many families were in attendance, and kids of all ages ran wild. Jamie sat with a group of single people on the edge of the chaos. Someone had brought a few bottles of wine and it was refreshing, even in the plastic cups.

The day offered many options—volleyball, badminton, football, horseshoes, and a variety of other picnic games. Jamie was content to sit on the side watching. She was enjoying the fresh air and the shrill laughter of the children.

As the sun set and the air began to cool, parents gathered their offspring. The families left and were replaced by joggers and walkers going about their evening routines. Jamie wasn't in a hurry to leave and had nowhere she had to be. She pulled a book out of her bag and leaned against the nearby oak to read. She sipped at the remains of her commandeered wine, making it last.

Occasionally she would look up to watch the men playing football. Now that the kids were gone, they had ditched their flags and were playing full-on tackle. Jamie was sure they would be limping at work on Monday.

She remembered playing football when she was in her teens. She was pretty good, too, until her dad informed her young ladies didn't play football. He wouldn't explain why, but after her first date with a quarterback, she understood their propensity for gaining ground wherever they could. She was then able to forgive her father's caution.

One player stood out from the rest. He talked a good game, harassing the older men in a fun-loving way. He was cocky but overall a good player. Her gaze kept drifting back to him unbidden.

Following a bad throw tipped wildly out of bounds, the ball landed at her feet. Jamie stood and picked it up. As she cocked her arm back to throw, Ben ran over within tossing range and held out his hands.

"I don't want you to hurt that lovely shoulder of yours," he said with mock chivalry.

Jamie gave him a deprecating look and let the ball fly. In a perfect spiral, it hit the quarterback in the chest, thirty yards away.

Nonchalantly, Jamie sat back down on the blanket and picked up her book.

Ben looked from her to the men on the field, all joyously cheering.

"Ben, stay there! Send her!" they yelled, laughing.

Shaking his head in disbelief, Ben returned to the field. Jamie noticed his game was altered. He wasn't catching at the same rate, and his mouth wasn't running as much.

She laughed to herself. The look on his face had been priceless. Now the gang continued to chide him for not being able to throw as well as a girl. Jamie tried to focus on her book but couldn't help sneaking peeks at Ben as the game continued.

Slender but with broad shoulders, he looked great in Dockers shorts and a drenched t-shirt. Jamie guessed his height to be about six feet, maybe taller. His dark blond hair was a little long at his collar and plastered to his face with sweat. Even from this distance she could make out the stubble on his baby face.

Several days later, Jamie sat in her office staring out the window. Over the last few days, her mind kept drifting back to the marketing director. She tore herself from her thoughts and spun her high-backed leather chair away from the window to face her desk.

The presentation had gone well but now she had to finalize the plans to carry out her recruitment drive. She began rifling through the paperwork her secretary had dropped in her basket earlier, looking for the accounting position resumes. She heard muffled voices from the entryway, followed by a quiet tap on her door.

A somber Ben Simons held a cup of coffee from the corner shop in front of him as a shield. Jamie smiled. "It's safe to enter."

Ben placed the paper cup on her desk. "I'm sorry I was daydreaming during your lecture. I did pay attention for most of it." He sounded like a reprimanded child.

"I hope so. There are a lot of things I need the marketing department to do."

"And we're fully on board, I promise," Ben confirmed.

They chatted a few more minutes; Jamie filled him in on the parts he had missed. Together they came up with a timeline and courses of action to reach their goal. Jamie was excited with the inputs Ben presented. He thought of some things she hadn't even considered.

"I'm sorry I called you out in front of everybody. It was out of line," she said. "I was annoyed with Kevin and took it out on you. That was unprofessional."

"No need to apologize. It was rude for me to let my mind wander. I will do my best not to let it happen again."

If Jamie had known what he was thinking, she wouldn't have been quite as quick to forgive him. Ben's mind had kept wandering back to that day in the park.

Of course, he had noticed her right away. She was dressed casually in long shorts and a plain t-shirt hugging her body nicely. Her hair was pulled back in a ponytail. He was playing football with the gang from the office and doing quite well, if he did say so himself—not bad for thirty-one. A few of the others playing were much younger.

He saw her look up a few times when the team cheered for a good play or a touchdown. Once, she spotted him watching her. He had turned away but knew he'd been caught. After that he tried to be more careful.

Ben watched Jamie smile and joke freely with her friends. When she laughed, she self-consciously covered her mouth with her hand. He thought it an odd gesture for such a beautiful woman.

The little kids loved her and brought her gifts of wildflowers or stones. She made a fuss over each gift and treated each child to a hug.

As people packed up to leave, he tried to think of ways to make sure she stayed. As it turned out, he needn't have worried. Jamie showed no sign of leaving. She pulled out a book. He was relieved and turned his thoughts to creating an excuse to talk to her.

His chance to approach her was realized when the football landed near her. Ben's attempt to compliment her backfired. She spiraled the ball past him, putting him in his place. He felt like a fool when he couldn't think of a good comeback. He walked away defeated. After that, his game was off. The harder he tried not to let his gaze drift to the oak tree, the worse he did in his game. Eventually he gave up and glanced back.

She was gone.

Chapter 3

Winkler and Stein Solar was a company on the edge of new solar technology. To stay ahead of the competition, the company needed to attract the best minds. They needed their name known in every household. That's how Jamie saw the link between marketing and human resources and growth for the company.

The U.S. Energy Secretary recently announced his support of Project Amp to put solar panels on industrial buildings across the country and tie them to the electrical grid. This solar generation project would include the installation of the same number of photovoltaic solar panels installed all over the U.S.—this time all under one project.

Jamie wanted to capitalize on the media attention given to solar energy as Winkler and Stein Solar bid for a piece of the contract. The first phase of the project would take place in southern California with additional installations being built in twenty-eight different states and the District of Columbia.

Project Amp was expected to produce enough energy to power tens of thousands of homes as well as significantly cut down on carbon pollution.

This was a great time to be a part of Winkler and Stein Solar, and she needed everyone to know it so they would be knocking down the doors to be a part of their company.

Jamie and Ben saw each other often as they worked together to refine her brainchild. She was glad they had come to a truce and was surprised to discover she even enjoyed his company. He saw Jamie's vision, and together they were able to put it into action.

Since they had begun working together, Jamie took notice of Ben more often around the building. He was a good-looking man and easy to spot. Being a social person, people naturally surrounded him.

As she watched him explain a concept to one of his subordinates, she admired his ability to connect with people. He didn't talk down to anyone and was willing to admit when he made a mistake. He handled himself quite well when she called him out during the training session for daydreaming. No excuses, just a simple apology and move on. He also didn't hold it against her.

It said a lot about his character.

But he wasn't a pushover either. He loved a collegial debate and held his own in dialogues to get his point across. He had mastered the art of allowing the other person to lose an argument with grace and come out of the discussion with both sides happy.

The subordinate Ben was talking to started nodding. Jamie saw the light coming on as Ben's concept solidified. A smile crossed his face, and he started talking with his hands as Ben folded his arms across his chest and smiled his encouragement.

His lack of self-centeredness was such a breath of fresh air, and she considered that the essential ingredient to any project team. She was concerned he was too transparent and… too good. She wondered how he had survived this long in the business environment where many would take advantage of such openness and use it for their gain. But he had made it this far, so he knew what he was doing.

He was well-respected, and Jamie knew from mutual friends in the human resource world that headhunters were trying to pry him away from Winkler and Stein. Although she didn't think he was actively seeking another job, she hoped he would stick around long enough to finish what they started.

Plus, she would like to get to know him more as a friend. She couldn't explain it and didn't want to try. She enjoyed the way he made her feel. His smile, quick wit, but also his ability to focus, made him extremely attractive.

Jamie knew her attraction to Ben was dangerous, and she needed something to distract her.

In addition to Ben, Jamie had another coworker she looked forward to seeing every day. Trina Roberts was a twenty-five-year-old brunette in the finance department. She adopted Jamie on her first day when she went in to file her W-4. Trina was fun-loving and kind. She had three sisters, but none were in the D.C. area, and she missed them terribly—hence, Jamie was designated a fourth sister. As an only child, Jamie was thrilled with this arrangement.

As if conjured from her thoughts, Trina stuck her head in Jamie's office. "Are you up for Pogo's on Saturday?"

Jamie choked on her coffee as a snort of laughter caught her off guard. "You've got to be kidding! Going out with you is dangerous."

"What do you mean? Pogo's is a nice respectable place."

"It isn't the place. You're a bad influence."

"Me? No way. I bring out the best in you."

"Like when you tricked me into going to a strip club?" Jamie challenged.

"I didn't trick you. You came along willingly."

"Because you sounded so depressed that your date stood you up. You didn't tell me where we were going."

"Watching men dance is a great way to forget being stood up," Trina said.

Jamie laughed as she recalled their last excursion.

After they had arrived and pushed their way toward the stage, Trina bought a round of drinks for the others sitting at the table in exchange for allowing her and Jamie to join them. The drinks arrived, and the lights went down.

As soon as the music started, Jamie realized her mistake. She experienced the thump-thump-thump of the bass through her chest. The lights began to flash, and the stage was suddenly alive with a half-dozen men in particularly tight clothing. As they swirled and worked the crowd, hundreds of women—and a few men—screamed in excitement.

"You're lucky there was no one there we knew," Jamie said.

"But your face was priceless when you turned to the stage in time to catch sight of a very firm ass encased in black directly in your sights."

Even thinking about it now, Jamie turned red with embarrassment. "I thought I was going to pass out when he ripped his leather pants off."

"There was nothing between you and a good time, except a few inches." Trina's eyes were watering from laughter.

"You will never again pick our outings," Jamie vowed.

"Come on. You'll be missing out."

"I'll wait for the cliff note version of your escapades." Jamie prized having a girlfriend to hang out with, but Trina was a little on the wild side compared to Jamie's mundane life. While Trina was very open and loved to share stories about her weekend adventures, Jamie was past those days and preferred not to discuss her personal life.

Trina had many male friends but not anyone serious. Watching Trina flit around during their excursions made Jamie feel much older than her thirty-three years, but Trina included her in all her undertakings and conversations. Jamie never felt left out.

"Your loss," Trina said as she headed back to her own workspace.

Jamie leaned back in her chair to take inventory of her life. Between her friends and work, things were very good since moving to Bethesda, Maryland. Her homelife was the only downside, as usual. She was hoping the move would make things better, but it didn't make a difference.

Looking on the bright side, she loved the access she had to Washington, D.C. She convinced herself, once the house was in order, she would take advantage of the free museums and cultural events. That was one area in her life where she felt she was lacking. Self-improvement was always on her to-do list.

In the meantime, she poured herself into her work.

Chapter 4

Jamie looked at the opulence around and wondered, not for the first time, how she got here. She had dropped her bags in her room and was now taking the opportunity to wander around the hotel as if it were a museum. She felt so out of her element in a place that made her best outfit look dowdy. The ladies walking through the lobby were long-legged and wearing heels. Jamie's feet hurt just looking at them.

The high ceilings were held up by beautiful marble columns. The gold frames adorning the walls held black and white photographs of Colorado Springs during its early days.

She glanced into the meeting rooms as she toured the hotel. The heavy drapes were pulled back to give an unobstructed view of the lake beyond. The large flower designs cut into deep, plush carpets weren't her style, although she appreciated the detail of work.

"Penny for your thoughts." Ben's voice cut into her musings.

"They aren't worth a penny," Jamie said sullenly.

Ben nudged her with his shoulder to make her smile. "Don't underestimate yourself," he said with a wink. "I'll pay you a quarter."

Jamie smiled and held out her hand. Ben slapped at it playfully.

"The women here are so glamorous," Jamie said, nodding toward the ladies by the outdoor bar. Their short skirts showed off the suntan they obviously spent time working on.

"You think?" Ben asked, following her gaze. "I think they're too fake. I mean, don't tell me those shoes are comfortable."

Jamie laughed. "That's not the point." She was secretly pleased they shared the same opinion.

"Then what *is* the point? Give me a woman who's comfortable in her own body any day. That's what I find sexy."

He said it so nonchalantly Jamie wasn't sure if he was serious or not. She started to laugh but stopped when he caught her eye.

"You are an anomaly," Jamie said.

"As are you, Jamie Woods. It's one of the things I like about you."

"One? You mean there's more?" Jamie dared.

"Much more." Ben nudged her once again. "Come on. Let's check out what's planned for this evening's events. Maybe it'll involve free alcohol."

Jamie fell in step with Ben as they went back through a set of glass doors into the hotel's foyer. "Every year the company drags us away to discuss the mission and vision for the future," Ben said. "Not sure how much we get accomplished, but they sure pick nice places for us to meet. That's incentive enough for us to keep our sales up. I've been to Hawaii and Las Vegas on the company's dime."

The Broadmoor in Colorado Springs was certainly the nicest hotel Jamie had ever been in. They had spas for adults, kids, and even pets. There were beauty parlors, barbers, clothing shops, gift shops, restaurants, and multiple bars. Jamie tried to take in all the activity as they walked through the lobby.

She stared out the extravagant main entrance to the driveway beyond. The light-colored brick walls formed a U-shape around the long courtyard—a very rich first impression as guests arrived at the hotel. Before coming on this trip, Jamie had read up on Colorado Springs. The Broadmoor had been built in 1890 to create an upper-class suburb of Colorado Springs with numerous amenities, including a casino.

It burned to the ground in 1897 but was rebuilt a year later. After regarding the extravagant structure, Jamie was surprised it had once been a girls' boarding school, at least for a short time before the Penrose family bought it in 1916 and set out to create the most opulent resort in the world.

Spencer Penrose was also responsible for the building of the Cheyenne Mountain Zoo. He used to keep animals on the resort grounds to amuse the guests, but the smell became too strong. As an alternative, he built them their own home nearby.

While she waited for Ben to check the schedule of events, she read yellowed news clippings framed on the walls.

In 1952, the hotel added sea lions to their lake to try to control the goldfish population. Guests complained about the noise, so the owners had to ship in saltwater fish to keep the sea lions satisfied and quiet. Apparently freshwater goldfish were not enough for their diet.

A bridal party sweeping through the glass front doors drew her attention. She watched as they made their way to the back of the building and the patio beyond. The bride actually glowed as she rested her hand on her groom's arm. Surrounded by her maids in waiting, she looked like the princess from a fairy tale. Jamie was sure a reception next to the lake would be one to remember.

"Looks like we're free until the mixer at six p.m.," Ben reported, having checked the schedule posted on the notice board. He looked around at the artwork on the walls.

"Did you know there's supposed to be a dancer with two right feet painted on the ceiling of the main mezzanine?" Ben asked.

Jamie wasn't sure if he was teasing her for being so interested in the history of the building, but she decided to bite. "Where?"

"I haven't found it yet, but we can go on a scavenger hunt. It'll be a challenge. Whoever finds it first, wins."

"What will I win?" Jamie asked.

"Don't go supposing you can beat me at my own game. I am a hidden object puzzle champion."

"You don't say?" she taunted. "In what grade?"

"Third, but I still reign! Want to discover a little of Colorado Springs?"

Jamie agreed. She wasn't used to being impulsive but didn't want to pass up this opportunity. She didn't travel much, although she had read many stories set in the Colorado Springs area. She wanted to see the sites with her own eyes. "Give me a chance to change. I'll meet you in fifteen."

Jamie threw her suitcase on the bed and unzipped it. She shook out her casual clothes, trying to find what was the least wrinkled. Trading in her blazer for a hunter green cardigan, she was more comfortable. She checked herself over in the full-length mirror to determine if the sweater made her look frumpy. Deciding it was the best of her options, she turned her attention to her shoes.

She was tempted to change into something nicer but didn't relish the idea of trying to keep up with Ben while wearing sandals. Her flats would have to do. She flung her camera over her shoulder and headed out.

When she left the air-conditioned building, the sun was warm on her face, and she had second thoughts about the sweater. Before she had a chance to go back inside, she heard a horn. Ben was waving from the driver's seat of a deep blue BMW Z20 convertible. Jamie laughed and walked toward him. The doorman reached the car before she did and opened the passenger door.

"Thank you," she said to the man as he smiled and closed the door.

"Have fun now," he replied.

Jamie looked at Ben as he shifted into gear and pulled away. He was grinning like a child with a new toy.

"You're unbelievable," Jamie said.

"Well, if you're going to be my friend, you'll have to get used to my quirks. One of which is my appreciation for the nicer things in life." He grinned at her. "Life is too short to settle."

Jamie relaxed in her seat and stared out the windshield at the majestic mountains around her. She had never seen such beautiful scenery. Pike's Peak had a bit of snow on it but wasn't covered. It was too late in the season.

"Where are we headed?" Jamie asked.

"Garden of the Gods—some of the most magnificent red rock formations in the states," Ben said. Jamie was glad she hadn't changed her shoes.

They drove past the visitors' center and found a spot inside the park to leave the car. It wasn't very crowded at this time of the evening but there seemed to be a few regulars conducting their workout routines. Jamie could tell they had been here before because they didn't carry cameras or stop to admire the scenery.

Jamie was in awe at the creations pushing out of the rocky soil around them. The path wound in and out of the mini mountains, giving the impression of seclusion around every bend, although there were other visitors hiking the trail.

"The rocks are red sandstone," Ben said as Jamie snapped a few photos. "The formations were fashioned by the erosion of the Ancestral Rocky Mountains, which were shaped during the Pennsylvanian Period about 300 million years ago. The red color is from the granites and gneisses from which it eroded. Scientists have even found aquatic fossils in these rocks."

"I didn't know you knew so much about rock formations."

"I started collecting rocks in elementary school."

"Could have been worse. Could have been bugs," Jamie quipped.

"That's what you find *under* the rocks," Ben said. Jamie rolled her eyes and walked on.

The hike was refreshing and the conversation interesting. Although they had been working together for months now, they rarely had the opportunity to talk about things other than work.

Now they talked about nothing and everything. Jamie revealed she was an only child of divorced parents. She didn't know what was worse, having two houses or not having a sibling to share them with.

"I'm still close to my mother. We talk a couple of times a week and email often. She lives in Richmond so we're making plans for her to come visit. I spent a few weeks with her before starting this job."

"Did she ever remarry?"

"Yep, to a wonderful guy. They're really happy."

"What about your dad? Do you stay in touch with him?" Ben asked.

She was habitually tight-lipped about anything in her personal life, but she found herself opening up to him.

"We aren't as close as Mom and I are, but he's a good dad. I was fortunate he stayed involved in my life while I was growing up. He always lived nearby so visitations were easier." Jamie smiled at a memory. "Sometimes that worked against me because Mom had her circle of spies, and Dad had his. I was never anywhere my parents didn't hear about."

Ben laughed. "It was my older sisters who would tell on me. At least until I was old enough to spy on them and their boyfriends. Then I had a little more leverage." Ben was the youngest with three older sisters and was admittedly spoiled rotten.

"My parents were married forty-six years. We lost Dad last year to cancer." Jamie heard the catch in his voice when he mentioned his father.

"I'm due for a visit to the ole homestead," Ben said in a poor western accent, walking with a swagger. Then he resumed his normal pace and voice. "I haven't been back for a while, but we all email a lot. I'm an uncle a couple of times over so I have to keep up on the latest stunts."

"And give them new ideas, I'm sure," she added.

He laughed, feigning an innocent expression.

Ben waited patiently as Jamie stopped to take pictures, appreciating the fresh air and the company. He offered to take her photo to send to her parents, but she declined. She was happy clicking away, looking for just the right angle. She enjoyed nature pictures most of all.

As the sun sank lower in the sky, Jamie was glad she had her sweater. They were getting in a good walk, but it was a slow pace, not like a workout.

Ben looked at his watch. "We better get going if we're going to make the ice breaker."

"Yes, I guess we should," she agreed. They turned and headed back toward the car, still not in a great hurry.

"I think we burned off enough calories for a beer or two," he said. "Or do you prefer wine?"

"I hear wine's good for you."

"Then wine it is!"

Chapter 5

They got back to the hotel in time for Jamie to grab a quick shower before she was expected at the mixer. She rushed to her room, dialing her cell phone as she walked.

"Hello?"

"Eddie, you won't believe how beautiful it is here!" She fumbled to slide her key card in the lock. "The mountains are gorgeous and—"

"Glad to hear it," Eddie interrupted. "Hey, can you tell me when you get back? I have some people waiting for me."

Jamie was crushed. She tried not to let him hear it in her voice. "Well, I guess I can tell you later."

"Thanks. Have fun. Talk to you soon." The phone went dead before Jamie had a chance to respond. He had never been one for chit chat, but Jamie never recalled him being so abrupt in the years they had been together. She tried to convince herself he would have taken more time for her if others hadn't been in the room. She wasn't sure it was true, but it was better than thinking things had gotten so bad between them that they couldn't even talk anymore.

She dropped her phone on the table near the TV and opened the minibar. For several seconds she contemplated her options. In the end, she decided to hold out for the wine downstairs. It was always less depressing to drink with others, and Ben had mentioned it was free.

When she arrived in the lounge for the mixer, the room was full. Winkler and Stein Solar had brought in senior executives from their branch offices around the world. Some people she recognized from their Washington, D.C. office, and others looked vaguely familiar. From video teleconferences, possibly?

She spotted Ben talking to two ladies from the Chicago branch. Jamie had met them a few months ago when they came to D.C. for training. She watched how attentive they were to Ben's every word. He laughed at something one of them said and reached out and touched her arm. Jamie tore her gaze away.

She made her way to the bar and ordered a glass of Colorado Sauvignon Blanc from the Holy Cross Winery. Taking her first sip of the cool, crisp flavor, she turned to examine the room. The wallpaper was accented in deep hues of a textured substance. It made you want to run your hand over it to feel the soft crushed velvet. The ceiling was painted light blue and wispy white like the sky on a perfect spring day. The illusion was broken by the borders of heavy wood beams every ten feet. It was still beautiful work, and Jamie found herself trying to make shapes out of the clouds.

"I'm going to run out of quarters," a voice whispered to her.

"Maybe you should save your lunch money," she said in a stage whisper without turning her head. Leaving Ben behind, she walked toward a vacated seat at a nearby table. Jamie introduced herself to her colleagues and the networking began.

A few glasses of wine later, Jamie inspected the buffet table to ascertain if anything was left. Not much to pick from, but she had to get something in her stomach. She put a few mushrooms, wilted celery sticks, and broccoli on a small plate and walked to the veranda for some fresh air. The night was chilly and the breeze off the lake was brisk.

Still, it was a nice, clear night and Jamie stared at the stars. She shivered.

"Allow me." From nowhere, Ben appeared, removed his jacket, and slipped it over her shoulders.

Jamie was grateful for the warmth and thanked him, not even bothering to wonder where he had appeared from. The faint smell of Ben wafted off the jacket. She snuggled into it like a child wearing her dad's coat.

"Get enough to eat?" She offered him food from her plate.

He waved it off. "No, thanks. Tempting to be sure, but I think you need it more. Let's find a place to sit." He led her down a stone walkway to a table, away from the noise emanating through the doors. He held out her chair as she settled herself.

Ben took the chair next to hers and took a drink from his glass. "Ready for a fun day of meetings tomorrow? We're going to learn how important we all are to the big picture."

"It's better than being in the office." Jamie popped a stuffed mushroom into her mouth.

"So, what do you think about working for Winkler and Stein?" Ben asked, leaning back in his chair and putting his feet on the seat next to him. Throughout their hike, work had never come up.

"I like it," she said. "It's challenging, and the people are great."

"Where did you work before?"

"For SAE."

"That's a pretty large mobility organization," Ben said, giving a nod of appreciation. "Didn't Hardy work for SAE?" Ben asked, speaking of their mutual boss.

"Yep." Jamie took a sip of wine. "He was the one who hired me fresh from college. I owe him a lot."

"Did you follow him here?" Ben grabbed a celery stick off her plate.

"He made me an offer I couldn't refuse. Working at Winkler and Stein is a great opportunity. How long have you worked for them?"

Ben did a quick calculation. "Five years, give or take. I worked for Macy's before that, in New York City."

"I'm impressed. Marketing for Macy's is huge."

"Yeah, but I was a small fish. At Winkler and Stein, I get a little more say in the big decisions." He looked out over the lake and sighed. "I like it here but give me the hustle and bustle of the big city any day."

Jamie stared dreamily at the mountains. "I've never been this close to mountains before. It's like a different planet."

"You need to get out more." Ben grinned.

She ignored his comment and took a deep breath. "The air is so clean here."

Ben followed her gaze. "Yeah, there's something about the mountains. When I was little, we used to go hiking a lot. It's an inexpensive pastime with a lot of kids." His thoughts drifted, and they were both silent for a while.

"Mom and I would go to the beach. Also an inexpensive pastime for a single mother," Jamie shared. "We would spend hours building sandcastles, even when I was too old for sand toys. The castles got more and more elaborate as I got older. We would build whole villages." A look of sadness swept over her face.

"What?" Ben asked. He had seen her expression change.

"It's nothing," Jamie said.

"Then share."

Jamie played with her drink glass, not meeting Ben's eyes. "Like any teenager, I turned into a brat. Mom had planned one of her outings to the beach, and I blew her off.

She had been making plans for weeks, even took time off work. Instead of coming straight home from school like I was supposed to, I left her a note on the kitchen table saying I was going to Dad's for the weekend."

"Ouch," Ben said.

"Ouch is right." She looked up and met his gaze. "On Sunday when Dad took me back to my house and found out what I'd done, he lit into me. It was the only time I remember him yelling. Usually he was on edge trying to be nice all the time. Mom was going to let it slide but Dad took my laptop away and insisted Mom ground me for a month. For the next month he would call out of the blue, just to see if I was home. Yep, he was pissed." She tapped on the side of her empty glass with her fingernails.

"All kids do stupid things, though. Even I had my transgressions."

"Do tell." Jamie rested back in the chair with her hands in her lap.

"Well, like I said, our family liked to hike. We were in West Virginia checking out our third waterfall of the day, and I started getting bored. Even though I was the youngest, I thought the girls were taking too long. They kept stopping to look at plants, toss rocks in the water, that sort of thing. I decided I would head off on my own."

"How old were you?"

"Ten or eleven. Old enough to know better. At first I stayed on the trail, but ahead of the rest of my family. Then I noticed a vague path leading closer to the falls, so I headed that way."

Ben mimed pushing branches out of his way and getting bit by mosquitos to make Jamie laugh.

She obliged. "Is there a bear in this story?" she asked.

"No, but that would make it more interesting." He considered it. "Pathetically, it was nothing so exciting. I wandered for a while but got turned around. I made my way to the edge of the waterfall and started to head back down. In the meantime, my parents had realized I was gone and panicked. They continued up the trail but didn't see the path I had taken. While they were going up, I was headed down."

Jamie shook her head, imagining the fear his parents must have endured.

"In the woods it got dark quickly, and I was afraid of falling in the river. I climbed up on a large boulder near the water still warm from the sun. I decided to stay put until I could decide what to do."

"You fell asleep."

"You guessed it. I feel asleep. To this day the sound of water makes me sleepy. The din also covered up the sound of their voices calling my name. I didn't wake up until my father grabbed me off the rock. Unlike you, it wasn't just a shouting match and a grounding. After mom decided I was unhurt, my dad busted my ass. I don't think I had ever been paddled like that before or since. Having to hike down the rest of the mountain with a bruised butt was double the punishment."

"You have to admit you deserved it," Jamie said. "Your poor parents!"

"My sisters felt sorry for me though. For weeks, they were extra nice to me. Sometimes they even slipped me extra dessert. All in all, it worked out for the best."

Jamie threw a broccoli stalk at him, which he caught in one hand and shoved in his mouth. "See? Women are still showering me with food!" he said.

She laughed at him. "It's getting late. I'm going to find a warm rock to fall asleep on." Leaving her plate and empty glass behind, she got up and started walking away, unsteady on her feet. She turned and tossed his jacket back at him before continuing on her way.

Chapter 6

The next morning, Jamie was refilling her coffee cup when Trina entered the hotel conference room. Jamie waved her over and poured her a cup. Trina dumped two packets of sugar into the black liquid and stirred. She sampled her creation and sighed. "All is now right with the world," she stated.

Jamie laughed. "Tough night?"

"Not really. I just have a hard time sleeping in a strange room. What about you? Last time I saw you, you were wandering out to the patio followed closely by Mr. Simons."

"Ben's a nice guy. Do you know him?"

"I've seen him around. He has a great reputation at work… and with the ladies," she said with a wink. "Everyone loves him."

"He talks a good game. I'm sure that's why he's good at selling things." Jamie saw the CEO move toward the podium. "Come on. We better get to our seats."

By the end of the meetings, Trina could barely keep her eyes open. "Jamie, I know you wanted to go out tonight, but I'm dead tired. I need to get some sleep, or I'm toast tomorrow."

Jamie was disappointed but sympathized with her friend. She walked her to the elevators and then headed out to the lobby to find out what the others were planning.

"Come on, guys," Jamie heard Ben say as she joined the group in the lobby. "How often do you come to Colorado Springs?"

"Really, Ben? The *zoo*?" one of the men teased.

"They have the largest giraffe collection in the states." Ben was pleading his case.

"Sorry. Count me out," a young woman with short red hair said. Her high heels and short skirt weren't made for roaming among the animals—well, maybe human animals.

"I'll go." Ben turned to Jamie standing behind him.

"Do you really want to?" he asked her but didn't give her a chance to change her mind. "We'll have to hurry. They close at eight."

"Let's go. I've got everything I need." Jamie's dress slacks and short-sleeve shirt were formal enough for the conference but also very comfortable. Plus, they allowed her to wear flats.

He guided her toward the front door and yelled back over his shoulder to the others, "Your loss. You won't learn the difference between a kangaroo and a wallaby."

They waved and Ben turned to Jamie with a huge smile. "Thanks. I would go by myself, but it's a lot more fun with someone else."

Jamie returned his smile. She was sorry Trina was too tired to join them but at least she wouldn't be sitting around the hotel all evening.

The valet brought Ben's rental around, and they were off on another adventure.

Walking through the front gate, Ben led them straight to the giraffes. Their habitat was large and held at least fifteen full-grown and a few baby giraffes. The walkway was built high so visitors could feed the animals. Ben shelled out the few dollars required to get a handful of lettuce leaves. He handed some to Jamie and approached the fence. With one hand he held out a leaf, with the other he stroked the animal's cheek. The long black tongue reached out and grabbed the leaf from his hand. Jamie laughed as Ben wiped his hand on his jeans.

"Your turn," he encouraged.

Jamie knelt down to give attention to the baby who couldn't quite reach the top of the fence. "Here you go, girl," she soothed. The baby took the offered food and continued to snoop for more. Jamie couldn't resist and fed her a few more leaves.

When she stood, Ben's large friend was finishing off the last of Ben's stash. Jamie handed Ben the rest of her food and concentrated on stroking the giraffe's long neck while Ben fed her.

"All gone," Ben said holding up his hands. The giraffe gave one last swipe with his tongue and moved on to the next group of visitors, his infatuation with Ben gone with the food.

"Let's go visit the elephants," Jamie suggested.

The smell was overpowering as they entered the elephant stalls. Jamie took shallow breaths to avoid breathing through her nose. A zookeeper was explaining to a group of young children how the elephant's ivory tusks were very strong but could still break off if hit hard enough. One of the elephants had a broken "tooth," the keeper explained. It didn't hurt unless it was broken off close to her mouth where the nerve endings were. He held out a piece of the broken ivory for them to touch. Jamie got in line with the children to feel the cold tusk.

After watching the keepers hose down an elephant for a while, they exited on the other side of the stalls. Relieved to be back in the clean air, Ben and Jamie happily trekked toward the lions.

The habitat was glass enclosed but the view was unbelievable. Two lionesses paced around two others stretched out on a large rock. One got tired of waiting and climbed on top of the prone pair, oblivious to their comforts. The smaller of the lionesses ceded her spot to the larger and hopped down.

Jamie was mesmerized by the large cats. She followed their graceful moves around the enclosure.

"I think you have an admirer," Ben said. Jamie turned her head and was surprised to be face-to-face with an exceptionally large feline through the glass. She jumped back startled. The cat eyes stared at Jamie, and she sensed there was a real thought behind them—besides food.

She stared back into the unusually large eyes, yellow-brown ringed in black. The irises looked like they had a wood grain with flecks of brown. The lioness' shady brown coat glistened in the sun. The wide mouth opened in a yawn, and the cat moved away from the glass, bored with Jamie.

Ben watched the interaction with fascination.

They moved on to the next exhibit. The engraved marker read Bengal Tigers, but Jamie didn't spot any signs of movement. She got as close to the enclosure as it would allow. Because of the high fence, she was unable to see into the moat directly below. She searched around for something to stand on.

Off to her right she spotted a short, wooden post holding a sign with some details about the captives. Placing the ball of her foot on the flat top, she hoisted herself up.

"I'm pretty sure that's not why they put the sign there," Ben said.

"Shhh, no one will notice." She braced herself on the chain-link fence and peered down.

"Mommy!" a small child screamed from behind them. Jamie flinched and lost her balance.

Before she had a chance to recover, Ben's hands were on her sides, steadying her. Her flesh burned where his skin contacted hers beneath the waist of her blouse.

Shakily, she stepped down from her perch as Ben guided her without breaking contact. When she had her footing, he turned her to face him. "I noticed," he commented.

Taken aback by his touch, she couldn't think of anything witty to reply. She simply said, "I still didn't find the tigers."

"Mommy!" the same voice cried out. "Look at the big cat!" the young boy jumped up and down excitedly pointing at a large boulder. Just beyond, the striped face of a golden feline peered out.

Jamie's eyes followed where he was pointing, and she spotted the tiger. Embarrassed over her near fall and not being able to spot what a child could see, she stared for a few minutes waiting for more. Her eyes were on the cat, but her thoughts were on the response her body had to Ben's touch. She could still feel the impressions his fingers made, although his touch was gentle. *This can't be right*, she scolded herself.

The sun was bright, but the breeze kept the air cool. As the sun dropped lower in the sky, Jamie rubbed her arms for warmth.

"It's getting chilly. Wait here," Ben said as he popped into one of the souvenir shops.

Jamie amused herself by looking at the key chains and snow globes in the doorway, wondering if Eddie would appreciate a gift from Colorado. Somehow, she doubted it.

A few minutes later, Ben came out with a shopping bag. From it, he pulled a long sleeve t-shirt and held it up for her to see. It featured a picture of two meerkats face-on, with what Jamie supposed were innocent expressions. A half-buried apple they were trying to hide was in the background. Ben handed it to Jamie. His thoughtfulness overwhelmed her, and she was delighted.

"It's so cute," she exclaimed, holding it up to examine the picture again. "Thank you!" She slipped the shirt over her head and immediately felt warmer. She was a little self-conscious about wearing a t-shirt with linen pants, but Ben didn't seem to mind so she wouldn't let it worry her.

"It looks great on you," he said, giving her the once over. "The innocent look is very fitting for you."

"What do you mean?" she asked with a smile in her voice.

"Oh, don't try to fool me. I'm on to your game."

"I have no idea to what you are referring," she said, placing an open hand on her chest in mock indignation, falling into the role of mistaken victim.

"You'll be found out, ma'am. You can't pull the wool over my eyes forever."

"Well, in that case, we should skip the sheep."

Ben shook his head dismissively. "That was bad—even for you," he laughed.

"On to the bears?" she asked.

"To the bears," he answered.

Chapter 7

The next day passed much like the one before. Motivational speakers opened the meetings, the CEO gave the next step in his vision, and then the larger body broke up into smaller working groups. Jamie and Trina went their separate ways after lunch—Trina to new customers, and Jamie to overseas expansion.

Jamie found a chair and put her purse and notepad on the table. After refilling her coffee cup, she walked back to her seat. She faltered when she saw Ben seated in front of her. She was concerned he'd get the idea she was following him and picked up her purse to relocate.

Ben spotted her. "Hey, Jamie. Having fun yet?" he asked.

Jamie set her coffee on the table and pulled out her chair. "It's interesting but I'm tired of all-day meetings."

"I've got another sightseeing trip planned for after work. You game?"

Jamie hesitated but only slightly. If Ben was getting the idea she was following him, he didn't let on or it didn't bother him.

"Sure, why not?"

The speaker began his opening remarks, and Ben turned to face forward. Jamie wasn't sure why she felt so uncomfortable about the idea of hanging out with Ben again. He was a great guy and a lot of fun. Too much fun? She wasn't sure.

Jamie walked along the knee-high stone wall. Out of the corner of her eye something splashed. She placed her backpack on the low wall and leaned over the barrier, staring intently into the water.

"There it is. Did you see it?" Jamie asked Ben. She leaned farther over the rail.

"There." She pointed again and looked at Ben. "You aren't even trying," she accused.

"Oh, yes I am," he said aloud, but then mumbled something under his breath.

"What?" Jamie asked. She was searching the water again.

Ben sidled up next to her, leaving only inches between them.

"Stop staring at me," Jamie said without pulling her eyes from the river. "You're making me blush."

"You're more interesting than the fish."

"I don't swim as well," Jamie admitted.

"Let's see." Ben grabbed her shoulders and playfully pushed her toward the water. She instinctively clutched his arms to keep from losing her balance. Ben laughed and righted her.

The spark that shot through her when she touched him was a jolt. She immediately released her grip and swatted his chest, trying to make light of her reaction.

"This isn't high school," she said, though she was laughing too.

"Come on." Ben picked up her pack and swung it to his back. "Let's climb to the top. It's only two hundred and twenty-four steps."

Jamie looked up to the top of Seven Falls. She didn't relish letting Ben discover how out of shape she was, but she couldn't back out either.

"After you," Ben insisted when they reached the bottom of the staircase, "and no laughing at me for being out of shape. Remember, the air is thinner here."

Jamie grinned, relieved Ben had given her a way out. She started up the steps, keeping a firm grip on the handrails.

"Stop looking at my butt," Jamie said without breaking stride.

"It takes my mind off the climb."

When they reached the first platform, Jamie turned Ben around and rummaged through her bag on his back. She pulled out her phone and circled to take in the view. The water fell in a more casual fashion than she expected. Its fall was broken along the way by many jagged outcroppings.

"It's magnificent," she said, snapping a few pictures from different angles. She did love the view, but it also gave her a chance to catch her breath.

At the top of the next set of steps, a path led away from the falls toward a pavilion. The shade housed benches made from half logs. Ben stumbled to one, dropped the pack, and stretched out on his back, throwing his arm up to cover his eyes.

Jamie studied him from the bench on the other side of the circle. His chest was heaving faintly from the exertion, and she enjoyed how his t-shirt clung to his torso. His jeans were faded and tight enough to highlight his quads without being out of style. Her eyes lingered for a moment too long where she had no business looking, and she felt her face flush. The skin on her stomach and sides where he had touched her at the zoo tingled.

The breeze felt wonderful, and Jamie closed her eyes to take in the delicious smells and sounds of the forest. She couldn't contain her smile. She was very happy. She couldn't remember the last time she felt this way with Eddie.

Feeling guilty, she opened her eyes to break her train of thought. Ben was in front of her, reaching out his hand.

"Daydream later. We have more waterfalls to see," he said.

The walk through the woods was a much more relaxing venture than the stairs, and they took their time. The dirt path was outlined with large boulders, and plenty of signs warned visitors to avoid the wildlife and stay on the trail. As they walked, their conversation meandered like the river they followed. They took advantage of the benches set at intervals along the way to rest and drink from the bottles of water Jamie had packed.

"What do you want to be when you grow up?" Jamie asked as they walked.

"Happy."

Jamie waited for more, but Ben didn't offer anything else.

"Happy?" Jamie asked. "What does that mean?"

"Just happy." Ben picked up a stone and tossed it into the stream. "I don't have any big dreams or career goals." He shrugged.

"You haven't even thought about it?"

"I like what I'm doing now. I'm not looking to climb the corporate ladder. My goals aren't in the business world."

She was confused. "Where are they?"

"Outside of the office. I want to make enough money to be comfortable and to travel. I don't want to lose myself in a career for the sake of having a career. I want to be confident enough to make the right decision. I want to marry my best friend and stay married forever. I want to have a few kids and spoil them rotten."

Jamie thought about his answer. He sounded pretty confident about everything, and she was convinced he'd find all he was looking for. He was that kind of man.

She wasn't sure she wanted to know the answer but had to ask. "Who's your best friend?"

"Don't know. Haven't met her yet."

Jamie was curious at the sense of relief his answer brought her.

"What about you? What do you want to be?" Ben asked.

She thought for a minute. "I'm not sure. It keeps changing. I like what I'm doing now but I don't want to do it forever. I'd like a more flexible schedule. Not sure where I'll be able to find that."

"It'd be great to have a flexible schedule as a parent. I think I'll add it to my list." He didn't look at her as he spoke, "Do you want to be a mom someday?"

"It's a scary thought, don't you think?" Jamie asked, not sure how to answer.

"In what way?"

"It's a lot of responsibility. They don't come with instruction manuals or anything."

"Oh, come on. Nothing could shake you. You face down bigger children every day."

"It's not the same." She grinned. "Not much shakes me but the thought of kids is daunting."

"You'd be a great mom," Ben said. "I've never seen you lose your cool. I'll bet nothing rattles you."

"You'd lose that bet! You just haven't figured out what it is yet."

"Do I hear a challenge?"

"Good luck," she said with a gleam in her eye.

Her thoughts drifted back to his original question. She had often dreamed of having children but felt she was running out of time. Eddie wasn't interested in kids, and she couldn't exactly do it alone. After a few more minutes of quiet contemplation, she answered, "I do want kids—more than one. I don't want to raise an only child. And I want to give them enough so they can explore their interests, but I don't think spoiling them is the answer. I want my kids to be respectful, polite, and intelligent."

"We are talking about kids, right?"

Jamie sidestepped enough to knock into his shoulder as they walked. He exaggerated his stumble and laughed.

He continued, "I believe in the nurture theory. Kids don't start out respectful and polite. It's all in how you bring them up. I think you can spoil them in the right way. I don't mean give them everything they want. You can give them everything they need, plus a little."

"How do you separate what they need from what they want? I mean beyond the basics of food and clothing. I can't stand those parents who hire tutors for their kindergartener so she can be the best finger painter in the class." She waved her hand in the air to dismiss the idea.

Ben nodded in agreement. "I don't want to use my kids to gain a competitive edge over the Joneses. But I do want to be able to give my kids the experiences I didn't have because we didn't have enough money. We weren't poor. But with four of us, to have us all doing extra activities would have been tough on the pocketbook."

Jamie conceded the point. "You have to give them time to just be kids. I don't want to be a parent who runs her children from event to event to give them a leg up. I want my kids to play with Legos, and cardboard boxes, and homemade puppets."

"Then it's settled." Ben climbed over a fallen log and reached back to help her over.

Jamie wasn't sure what he was referring to but didn't ask. She just enjoyed the innuendo, and they lapsed into a comfortable silence.

After a few minutes, Ben said, "Now I have to think of what rattles you." He flashed her a grin. "The challenge is on."

Chapter 8

On their way back to the Broadmoor, Ben and Jamie were content to admire the scenery and large houses they passed. They pointed out particularly remarkable mansions as they wound their way along back streets, not in a hurry to get back to the hotel.

"Just look at that house," Jamie said dreamily as they drove past a large Spanish style house with a For Sale sign in the yard. "Can you imagine what it would be like to live there?" The black rod iron gate gave the house a protected feel without blocking its beauty from the street.

Ben slowed the car. Grinning, he opened his cell phone and dialed a number. He read the name from the realty sign as they drove past. "Hello. I'm looking for Ms. Oaks." After a short pause, he continued in a stern voice, "Ms. Oaks, we had an appointment. You might not think my time is worth much, but I do." He waited while Ms. Oaks spoke. "We're sitting in the driveway of 11201 Cheyenne Mountain Drive, but you aren't here." He paused again.

Jamie could imagine the woman shuffling through papers trying to find evidence of their appointment.

"We don't have much time. We're only in town for the day. We need to fly back to D.C. this evening. I'll tell my assistant to find a more reliable real estate agent next time— " He listened again. "You know, forget about it. If you don't—" He paused again. "That will do. We'll see you in ten minutes." Ben closed the phone and did a U-turn.

"What did you just do?" Jamie asked in wonder.

"Got us an appointment to check out the house," Ben answered matter-of-factly. He pulled into the circular driveway and put the convertible in park. "Let's check out the grounds while we wait."

Jamie sat in stunned silence while Ben got out of the car and walked around to her side. He opened the door, offering his hand. "Shall we?"

She couldn't believe she was going along with this. The house was incredible. It was like a fairytale castle. The two-stories were sunset pink stucco with red Spanish tiles on the roof. With four off-white marble columns holding up a smaller pitched roof, the front entrance came out to greet guests. The immaculate landscaping must have kept numerous gardeners busy around the clock; the shrubs in the front were cut low to the ground forming a rounded design around the pathway from the driveway.

On both sides of the entrance on the upper floor, symmetrical terraces jutted out, framed in black rod iron. The baby blue shutters added a touch of color against the pale pink. They made their way around the right side of the house. Jamie's breath caught as she took in the unobstructed view of the mountains. The back lawn was a sea of green bordered by large red rocks marking the boundary. Beyond the rocks, the land dipped and stretched out to the mountains ahead. Jamie saw a herd of antelope in the distance. She almost cried in delight.

Ben grabbed her hand, pulling her back toward the house. "You have to see this patio."

The flagstone was laid with an intricate, random pattern. A large stone chimney was along one side with a built-in gas grill. A table with twelve chairs sat invitingly nearby. Long, curved bay windows reached out to the patio with a terrace above matching the contours. A white, wooden bannister kept those on the upper floor safe.

Ben heard a car drive up. "Let's meet her out front. I want to get the feel as we walk through the main entrance."

Jamie followed Ben, still in disbelief they were actually going inside. As they rounded the corner, Jamie saw the real estate agent examining the BMW. "My wife and I have got to catch our jet tonight, or the boss will kill me. He only said we could borrow it for one night. I'm Ben," he said, extending his hand, "and this is Jamie."

Jamie shook her outstretched hand, still reeling from Ben's casual tone when introducing her as his wife.

"I'm sorry about the misunderstanding," the real estate agent said, shaking their hands. "My name is Patti. When are you looking at moving?"

"The sooner we can close, the better. We just accepted an offer on our place in Georgetown, so the timing is perfect."

"Let's go inside, shall we?" Patti led the way up the walk, calculating her commission already, Jamie was sure.

Ben placed a hand on Jamie's lower back and guided her to the tiled portico. Patti unlocked the door and stood aside to allow them an unhindered view into the entryway.

The white tile gleamed spotless, drawing the eye up the matching marble columns to the tall windows at the rear of the house. Jamie entered as if walking into a dream. The high ceilings and spiral staircase were picture perfect. Ben moved ahead and opened the glass doors to the balcony beyond.

The balcony wasn't very wide, but cushioned chairs were arranged with a beautiful view over the yard to the mountains beyond.

"Can't you imagine sitting here with a cold beer and a good book?" Ben said. "What a great way to unwind after a long day."

Below was an open courtyard with dusky paving stones surrounding a fountain. Strategically positioned patio furniture allowed for smaller, more intimate gatherings.

Jamie took in the view over Ben's shoulder. She could imagine the amazing parties this palace could host.

She went back inside and rounded the staircase to the left, entering the kitchen area. The whitewashed cabinets and light oak-stained hardwood floors gave the room an open feel. The island had a raised area for casual seating on high-back bar stools. There were two ovens and a five-burner stovetop in stainless steel. Jamie was in heaven. A wine refrigerator was conveniently stocked and set at the perfect temperature.

"Jamie, come see the study," Ben called from the other room. She followed the sound of his voice and entered a room with floor to ceiling bookshelves in dark wood. With the brown tile flooring, the room was as dark as the kitchen was light and had a rich feel to it. Jamie loved it instantly.

Off the study were double doors leading into the master bathroom. The shower was spacious with two showerheads and beautifully etched flowers on the glass covering from knees to shoulders. The Jacuzzi tub could fit two people and had a view into a rock garden surrounded by trees for privacy. Candles were placed around the edge of the tub.

"Add a few ferns in here, and this could be your own private oasis," Ben whispered in her ear.

Jamie smiled, picturing herself lounging in the tub full of bubbles. She blushed and turned away when she envisioned Ben soaking alongside her. Only then did the thought of Eddie creep into her mind.

She walked through the bathroom into the master bedroom. This room alone was bigger than her living area and bedroom combined at home. The large canopy bed was situated to take in the view through the large glass doors.

Decorated in all white—carpet, walls, and drapes—the room was too stark to be cozy. In front of the white marble fireplace were two chaise chairs, also white, but decorated with colorful throw pillows. She didn't imagine the fireplace had ever been used in such a pristine environment. When she looked closer, she recognized the fake logs of a gas fireplace.

Ben and Jamie continued their tour through the house, pointing out things they liked and disliked. Ms. Oaks hung on their every word. After an hour and a half, Ben shook the agent's hand, accepted her card, and said they would be in touch. He led Jamie out and opened the car door for her.

Jamie was giddy with excitement as they drove away. She hadn't had that much fun in years. It reminded her of playing dress up when she was a little girl, trying on her mom's beautiful clothes and fancy jewelry.

Ben was also grinning ear-to-ear. "I think it's a little small, don't you?"

As they laughed together, Jamie realized how good it felt to simply enjoy life. She was comfortable with Ben, and even the lapsed silence didn't make her antsy to fill it.

She looked at the beautiful neighborhoods they passed through. When she was little, she and her mom played a game where they made up stories for the people behind the doors.

She pointed at a large house and said, "He inherited a lot of money and bought this big house. Now he wants to fill it with kids, but his wife would rather take tennis lessons at the country club."

Without missing a beat, Ben added, "He may want kids but he's compensating for small private parts, which is why he bought such a big house to begin with. The tennis instructor, on the other hand…" He let the sentence die and finished it with an exaggerated wink.

He pointed at a Tudor-style house set back from the road with a tree-filled front yard and manicured lawn. "Now this guy has it right. He married money. His wife is a doctor. While she's at work all day, he putts around outside with his lawn toys, contemplating what he'll buy next."

Jamie smiled her agreement. She was pleased he caught on so quickly. She spotted a house surrounded by a high stone wall. "They have issues. Trying to keep people out or lock someone in?"

"Tough call."

"What kind of house do you want?" she quizzed, her eyes still searching the lots.

"Not too big," he answered thoughtfully. "I like big rooms and open spaces. Lots of windows."

"I want a gym in my house, so I don't have to sweat in front of other people," Jamie said.

"Privacy is good, but I still want to live in a neighborhood. I want my kids to have friends to play with."

"I think the kids should have a separate playroom from their bedroom. They need a place they don't have to clean up every day, but I think their rooms should be neat."

"Please don't say you want them to make their beds every day!" Ben groaned.

"No way. I don't even make my bed."

"Thank God." Ben laughed.

"But they should have their share of chores."

"Agreed."

"And no car when they turn sixteen."

"What if your son wants to take a girl on a proper date?" Ben asked.

"He can borrow mine, after he washes it and fills it with gas."

"Nice. Slave labor."

"He can always take the bus."

Ben pulled into a parking space at the hotel, and Jamie was sorry their role playing had come to an end.

Chapter 9

As Ben ordered their third round of drinks, Trina slid into the booth next to Jamie, and he added her drink to their order.

"You look cute," Trina said to Jamie.

Jamie blushed at the compliment and finished off her drink. She had changed into a taupe silk blouse and a knee-length skirt in honor of such a beautiful evening and stuck to sandals. She wondered if Ben had noticed.

"So, how were your adventures today?" Trina asked.

Jamie and Ben exchanged a look.

"Okay, what did I miss?" Trina persisted.

"Just a tour of the most gorgeous house you could imagine. Ben is thinking about putting down a deposit," Jamie said with a hint of humor in her voice.

Trina stared open-mouthed at Ben. "Out here? Why?"

Ben laughed. "She's pulling your leg. We were having a little fun dreaming of hitting the lottery."

The drinks came. "Here's to winning the lottery," Trina said with her glass raised. They all clinked glasses.

As Jamie animatedly described the house to Trina, she felt something brush against her leg. Thinking she had bumped Ben sitting across from her, she adjusted her sitting position and continued her conversation.

As Jamie described the rolling back lawn, Ben interjected, "It would be such a *challenge* to mow."

The ladies looked at him curiously, but Jamie shrugged him off and went on with her story.

This time she was sure it was no accident. She felt a light touch on her bare leg. She glanced at Ben and saw him intensely watching her over his gin and tonic, a slight grin on his face.

Jamie felt her face flush. She wasn't sure if it was the alcohol or the intimate touch from Ben shooting electricity through her body. She was having trouble concentrating.

She took another sip of her drink and began describing the grounds. They were too elegant to call a yard, and she got excited again in the telling.

As the inside of his foot caressed her calf, she was flustered and then recalled their conversation on the hiking trail. *Dammit, he's messing with me on purpose,* she thought. She fought to maintain her composure and continue her monologue.

Thankfully, after only a few more questions, Trina shifted her questions to Ben. Jamie felt the touch on her leg stop moving. He shifted in his seat as he answered her queries.

Jamie allowed herself to relax for a moment before going on the offensive. The alcohol was taking hold, and she rationalized her actions as harmless fun.

Ben continued the thread of the discussion. Jamie kicked off her shoe, crossed her legs, and brought her foot into contact with Ben's upper thigh. He stuttered in his description of the patio but cleared his throat and resumed his description. He made it through Trina's quiz of the house before glancing in Jamie's direction.

She raised her eyebrows. *Not so easy now, is it?* her look conveyed. As Ben began to take a sip of his drink, she said, "Getting into the house was quite a challenge."

Ben choked back laughter and spilled some of his drink on his shirt. He dabbed at it with a napkin Jamie tossed at him.

Jamie tortured him a while longer by running her bare foot along the inside of Ben's thigh. When she started to feel herself getting aroused, she decided it was time to call it a night.

"Well, enough fun for me, folks," she said as she inconspicuously slipped her shoe back on and stood. She patted Ben on the shoulder as she walked by him. "I'll see you at breakfast before we catch the airport shuttle." She gave a wave and was gone.

Ben tried to focus on what Trina was saying, with little success.

Jamie wasn't ready to sleep. The alcohol had lowered her inhibitions, and Ben's fancy footwork had thrown her over the edge. Now she lay on her bed, thinking about him.

She got up and stepped in front of the full-length mirror on the bathroom door. She examined her reflection and let her fingers outline the opening of her blouse. She unbuttoned it, fantasizing she was undressing for Ben.

As she let her blouse fall open, she admired the curve of her breasts. Not bad for her age. She was still confident in her figure, just not in her ability to brandish it in the best way. She kept her blouse on, enjoying the silky feel of the fabric. She worked the skirt over her hips and let it fall to the floor.

Back in his room, Ben stripped off his shirt. He needed a cold shower to combat the massive erection that had been building up all day. Seeing Jamie's bare legs had tipped the scales. He had been fighting his conscience on whether to push the bounds of their friendship.

Trina's entrance had derailed his plans, but he used her distraction as an excuse to entice Jamie a little more. When she turned the tables on him, he didn't think he'd escape without embarrassment.

Now safely in his room, he let his thoughts wander where they had been going all week. He was dying to feel her arms around him. Every time he saw her smile, he wanted to taste her lips. *Dammit!* He wanted to taste all of her. He groaned and headed into the bathroom.

Ben was waiting in the lobby, coffee in hand. A group of people from the D.C. office were milling about, waiting to catch the shuttle.

Jamie was embarrassed over her actions the previous night so decided to take breakfast in her room. She wasn't sure how to act toward Ben. As she rolled her suitcase out of the elevator, she spotted him and felt her face grow red. He saw her and waved her over.

He was in the middle of a conversation when she joined the group, and she fell in silently. They were back into business mode early this morning. She listened with one ear while thinking about all the things she needed to do when she got home.

The others wandered off to refill their coffee, leaving Jamie and Ben standing alone.

"Thanks," he said.

"For what?"

"For hanging out with me. It was fun. It made a business trip a lot less boring."

She smiled. "I had fun too. Thanks for being my tour guide and chauffeur."

"Anytime. Speaking of which, I have to go so I can drop the car off at the rental place before the flight." Almost as an afterthought, he asked, "Do you want to ride with me?"

Jamie shook her head. "Not this time. This suitcase would never fit. Besides, I already promised to have a latte with Trina. Thanks though."

Was that disappointment in his eyes? Jamie couldn't be sure.

"I'm home." Jamie's voice echoed in the empty house.

She pulled her rolling suitcase through the kitchen and down the hall to her bedroom.

The bed was unmade, and dirty clothes littered the floor.

Jamie felt a mixture of relief and irritation in the same moment. Eddie wasn't at home, so she didn't have to play happy to see him, but he also knew when she was getting home. He could have been here waiting. Or offered to pick her up at the airport.

She tossed her suitcase on the bed and went through the motions of unpacking. She pulled out the t-shirt Ben bought her at the zoo. Hugging it to her chest, she briefly wondered what Ben was doing. Was he thinking of her?

She threw the shirt back into the suitcase. Knowing she had to dismiss the fantasy she had been living the past week, she tried to look toward the future. Perhaps she had time to run to the store to pick up ingredients for Eddie's favorite meal.

Chapter 10

Monday morning Jamie took extra care getting dressed for work. She held up one blouse after the other as she tried to decide what to wear. The castoff items piled on the floor. Although her selection of clothes was sizeable, almost everything she had was stern and business-like. She wanted something softer and sexier… but still office appropriate.

Eddie hadn't come home until after Jamie had gone to sleep. He was up and gone before her alarm went off but didn't bother to wake her or even leave a note. Again, she felt relief followed by guilt for not wanting to face him.

The clock chimed in the hall, and she knew she couldn't dally any longer. She settled on the cranberry blouse with a fitted black skirt. She made the decision to put on pumps rather than her usual flat shoes. A short pearl necklace topped off the outfit.

Jamie wasn't much on makeup, but she did add some color to her cheeks and put on a touch of mascara. She didn't want to go overboard. Taking one last look in the mirror, she rushed out the door.

When she arrived at the office, she tried to appear casual as she kept her eye out for Ben. Jamie was disappointed when she made it all the way to her office without a Ben-sighting.

Ben discarded the khaki slacks as too wrinkled and picked up a dark gray pair. If he hung them in the bathroom as he showered, the steam should work.

He hastily showered and took his time shaving. He didn't want to get to work with toilet paper sticking to cuts on his chin.

He considered aftershave but decided against it. He didn't want to be obvious. Buttoning up his white pinstriped shirt and adding a maroon tie, Ben checked his appearance in the mirror. Was he over doing it? His watch beeped on the hour, and his decision was made—it would have to do. He didn't want to be late.

As Ben pulled into his parking space behind the four-story, gray brick office building, he noted Jamie's car was already in her spot in the next row. He picked up his briefcase and headed into the building, casually scanning for her. He glanced through the glass doors into Jamie's office area and saw a young woman with shapely legs talking to Jamie's secretary, Carolyn. He slowed down to look past them into Jamie's office. His mind fought to sort out the characters as the woman laughed and walked around the desk toward the office. It was Jamie! Ben had to force himself to keep moving as Carolyn gave him a questioning look.

Ben was still off balance as he entered his own office and sat behind his desk. He couldn't remember ever seeing Jamie wearing heels. *Incredible legs!* Ben felt his mind drifting and his body responding, so he reined himself back in and turned on his computer, determined to get some work done.

Jamie walked into the large conference room and took her assigned seat on the right side of the oval table. She glanced around at the thick, blue carpet and the pictures on the wall. Primarily they were framed news articles about the company's successes. One wall displayed the many awards and achievements Winkler and Stein had accumulated over the years. Against three of the walls, empty chairs with faux, light-blue leather awaited guests for large meetings.

She greeted people as they entered and tried not to appear as if she were looking for someone. Her gaze kept drifting back to the door as she completed her pretense of an inspection of the room. The twenty-one chairs around the large table were laid out with ten on each side, leaving one end open to the screen in the front of the room. On the opposite side facing the screen, another chair matching the others was reserved for whoever was leading the meeting. It was a conscious decision to make it match the other chairs to exude the team approach Winkler and Stein very much endorsed.

Only minutes before the morning staff meeting began, Ben rushed into the room and took his seat across from Jamie. He caught her eye and smiled at her. She smiled and glanced away.

Steven entered the room, and as expected, said, "Let's get this party started."

Throughout the meeting, Jamie's eyes kept drifting to Ben. A few times, he caught her looking at him and smiled in return. Jamie felt her face flush. She took copious notes to keep her mind focused. It wasn't helping.

She was dying to talk to Ben but wasn't sure what to say. She couldn't think of a good excuse and didn't want to appear like a tongue-tied schoolgirl. The next moment, she was feeling guilty for even thinking of Ben as more than a colleague.

At the end of the meeting, she slipped out through the closest exit. She hurried back to her office and shut the door behind her. She leaned against it, feeling relief in the solitude. And feeling silly.

Ben was sure Jamie caught him staring at her but at least she smiled at him. He wasn't sure what to expect. There was definitely a connection there, but he didn't know what to make of it. Oh, what was he going on about? There was no chance there.

"Ben," his boss interrupted his thoughts. "Can you give us an update on your plan for the northwest? When will the ad campaign be ready to kick off?"

Ben concentrated on answering the question. He could sense Jamie's eyes on him but didn't dare look her way.

After the meeting, his boss stopped him to chat about the results of the working group he attended the week previous. Ben tried not to appear agitated as Jamie slipped out the door.

Jamie was thankful when the day was over. It hadn't felt like she accomplished anything, and the hours had dragged on. Her feet were killing her from wearing heels, and she wanted to relax in her pink slippers. The thought of getting home and opening a bottle of wine accompanied her out of the building. She walked out the employees' entrance at the back of the building to her car, lost in thought.

"Hey, you," Ben said.

Jamie started. Ben must have come out a different exit, and she didn't see his approach.

"Do you miss Colorado as much as I do?" Ben asked, walking closer.

Jamie searched Ben's face for a hidden meaning to his words but didn't find one. "I do prefer the Broadmoor," she answered.

He paused in front of her and smiled. "We only have to wait another year to escape again."

Jamie blushed because she had already pulled up the company calendar for the next off-site schedule. She made an effort to free her keys from her purse.

Ben continued walking to his car.

Jamie noticed his gray Toyota Camry for the first time. "What happened to your love for fancy cars?" she asked.

Ben slowed his pace. He laughed. "Well, the only way to afford to live the good life is to be practical the other days."

Jamie couldn't argue with that. She was a very practical person, sometimes to a fault.

"Someday it'll all pay off," he said, reaching his car. "See you tomorrow."

"Okay." Jamie lifted her hand in a half wave. "Tomorrow, practical man."

He smiled in return and the image lingered with her as she slid into her own car.

Chapter 11

The next morning, Jamie was back in her usual sensible clothes and shoes. She visited the company cantina for her morning coffee rather than using the one in her office. She glanced around for a sign of Ben. She had just filled her coffee cup and was adding the creamer when Trina approached.

"Glad you survived the conference," Trina said, pouring herself a cup.

Jamie gave her a sideways glance, wondering what she suspected. Seeing nothing challenging in her manner, she answered, "It was great." And after a slight hesitation she added, "The meetings were okay too."

Trina smiled. "I know what you mean. I love being paid to go on vacation, and that's exactly what those off-sites feel like to me, once I adjust to the hotel mattresses." She stirred her coffee. Without looking up, she asked, "What do you think of Ben?"

Jamie decided she needed more sugar and busied herself with refilling the sugar bowl. She tried to sound casual. "He's a nice guy. Very good at his job. Well respected."

"And he's hot," Trina supplemented.

Jamie almost dropped the sugar bag she was putting back into the cupboard. When she recovered, she said, "Don't you think he's a little old for you?"

"No way. Experienced guys are the way to go. Besides, what man could resist a younger woman?" Trina batted her eyelashes and flung her hair back dramatically.

Jamie liked Trina but the idea of her with Ben was unsettling. Trina kept up the charade by tilting her head seductively, letting her hair fall over one eye. "Look into my eyes," she crooned in a mesmerizing voice, "you will soon find me irresistible."

Jamie had to laugh. She was right. Ben would fall all over Trina.

On Wednesday, Ben approached Jamie in the cafeteria. She was reading by herself in the corner of the large room as she ate her lunch. The steady hum of conversation provided background noise without distraction.

"Mind if I join you?" he asked.

"Of course not." Jamie indicated a seat. Her heartbeat quicken.

Ben pulled out a heavy plastic chair on metal legs and settled himself. He examined the contents of his tray.

"Trying to decide where to start?" Jamie asked.

Ben grinned. "Decisions, decisions."

For a moment, their eyes met, then Jamie found something incredibly interesting on her own plate.

Ben dug into his lunch. After a short, uncomfortable silence he said, "Some of the guys are going to the Liberty

Tavern after work on Friday. It's turned into kind of a tradition, but I've never seen you there."

"Trina's mentioned it before. It's not my thing."

"Come on. You need to at least give it a try."

"Oh, I don't think so," she said, unsure.

"It's a great way to get to know folks. And you'll find some work is better accomplished over a beer."

Jamie pushed the food on her plate around with her fork. "We'll see."

"I can give you a ride if you want," Ben offered. "That way you don't have to worry about drinking and driving."

"No," she answered a little too quickly. "I'll be okay to drive."

From the twinkle in his eyes, Jamie could tell Ben took her answer to mean she would be coming.

Now what have I gotten myself into? Jamie wondered.

Friday night, Ben leaned against the heavy wood of the bar and watched the door for Jamie's arrival but continued to be disappointed. Every time someone new entered and it wasn't her, he got more irritable.

His heart jumped when he felt a hand on his shoulder. His smile faded when he turned to find Trina standing behind him. He recovered swiftly and flashed her a grin.

"Hey, Trina. What can I get for you?"

Trina let her hand slip from his shoulder down his arm without breaking contact. "A beer would be great."

Ben turned back to the bartender, slipping out of her grasp, and ordered a beer for her and a gin and tonic for himself. He grabbed them from the bar and motioned toward an open tall table against the wall, giving him a view of the door. Trina led the way. Ben watched her tight jeans and had to appreciate her figure.

As they chatted, Ben was still distracted. Trina was very friendly and talked non-stop. She touched his hand often as she made a point and continued to slip closer to him, using the excuse that it was hard to hear with all the noise of the crowd. Ben couldn't mistake her intentions, but he wasn't interested in her. She was too young and more interested in the "right now" rather than any look toward the future.

Future? Ben thought. *Not like my situation has any future aspirations.*

After his fourth drink, he decided to call it a night. Trina was visibly disappointed and tried to convince him to stay. She took his hands in hers and moved in even closer. Ben could smell the beer on her breath and knew she had put away quite a few tonight. "Want to walk me home?" she asked.

Ben knew if he agreed, she wouldn't stop pressuring him at the front door, and he didn't need the drama.

"Trina, I'm tired and need to go. Do you want me to call you a cab?"

Her face flashed annoyance, but she doubled her efforts. She stroked his hand and circled his thumb with her thumb and forefinger. "Are you sure?"

He gave her hand a quick squeeze and released it. "I'm more interested in sleep. Let me call you a cab."

Trina sat back and crossed her arms in a pout. "I'll be fine, thanks."

Ben made his escape. When he looked back through the dim light, he saw Trina had picked up her beer and joined a group in the back of the bar. She was already laughing.

He brooded all weekend. Of course, she never said she would come, but she did imply it. Maybe she was messing with him. Or maybe she didn't think twice about him. Ben was frustrated with his preoccupation over the topic.

He enjoyed Jamie's company more than anyone else he knew. She was intelligent, good looking, and had a sharp wit. He appreciated that combination in a woman. Most women his age tried too hard: trying to meet the right guy, trying to be on their best behavior, trying to be a good catch. It frustrated Ben. He wanted to meet someone who was natural and fun to be around. She didn't have to be the most attractive woman in the room, and she needed to be real with him. He hated playing the dating games.

His mind drifted back to Jamie. He thought they were friends, but maybe he was wrong. Maybe his problem was he just thought about her too much.

Chapter 12

Monday morning staff meeting was a challenge. Ben usually looked forward to the chance to see Jamie, but now he didn't know what he thought or felt. He should act like her blowing him off didn't matter. No point in acting hurt. It may reveal too much about his feelings. He was sure if he talked to her, she would sense it in his tone. He avoided looking in her direction. He left the conference room as soon as the meeting concluded and went to his car. He needed some fresh air.

"So how was Liberty Tavern on Friday?" Jamie asked Trina as they set their lunch trays on the table.

"It was fun. You should have been there," Trina answered.

"I know. I wanted to be," Jamie said. "My mom sounded awful when she called, and I was worried. Good thing I went. I ended up taking her to the emergency room in the middle of the night. She was having trouble breathing."

"How's she now?"

"Better. They released her on Saturday after running a lot of tests. She had the onset of pneumonia, but we caught it in time. My stepfather returned from his business trip on Sunday so she's in good hands."

"Did Eddie go with you?"

"Are you kidding? He had a dart game, and he couldn't let his team down."

"Are you shitting me?" Trina's eye widened.

Jamie shook her head. Eddie's choice to be with his friends rather than her had stung, but it was also a relief to be away from him. She felt like she was constantly tiptoeing around, trying not to set him off for something random.

Thankfully Trina decided to let the matter drop. "Your parents are lucky you live so close."

"But not too close," Jamie added. "I don't think it's healthy to live closer than a few hours' drive of your parents."

Jamie adored her mother. Betty Reilly was spunky and full of adventure. At fifty-nine, she kept her figure by exercising regularly. Even though her first marriage hadn't worked out, Betty didn't let it spoil her outlook on life. She had created many adventures to share as Jamie was growing up. Sometimes they would simply be going to the airport to ride the terminal trains and watch the airplanes land. As Jamie got older, they would jump into the car and just drive, stopping at any interesting points they saw. It might be a museum or an old church. Betty was open to suggestions and never treated Jamie's opinion as if it didn't matter. They always found a hotel with a pool, and Betty would get in with Jamie more often than not. They would hit a beach ball around, splashing each other more like friends than mother and daughter.

Betty had remarried just before Jamie graduated high school. At the time, Jamie was a little jealous, but by then she had her own friends and her own life she left her mother out of. It was only fair her mom found someone special, and Bob was perfect for her.

"Fill me in on Friday. Who generally goes to these things?"

Trina continued to share stories from Friday night. There had been a pick-up pool tournament that raised a lot of money for "charity," she said using her fingers as quotations when she mentioned charity.

Jamie laughed. She caught movement out of the corner of her eye and saw Ben enter the lunchroom. She raised her hand in a wave, but Ben didn't see her. He picked out his food, paid for it, and left.

Wonder what he's working on that has him so preoccupied, Jamie thought.

By Wednesday, Jamie was no longer making excuses for Ben dodging her. He had been avoiding her for three days. If they were going to be friends, she needed to treat him as a friend and figure out what was bothering him.

When Ben walked out of the building at the end of the day, Jamie was leaning against his car.

"Hey, practical man," Jamie said, trying to overlook Ben's hesitation she perceived when he spotted her.

Ben paused and then continued his approach. "What's up?" he asked.

"Visited any zoos lately?"

"No time," he answered.

"Ben, what's up with you?"

Direct. Add it to the list of things Ben liked about her. "I've been busy, that's all. The program you've outlined has added a workload I didn't budget for."

"You mean the program I outlined, and you signed up for?" Jamie said with a smile. "Don't tell me you took on more than you can deliver," she said. She was well outside her comfort zone playing the flirt but was trying her best to recapture the feeling they had shared in Colorado and get herself out of her funk.

"I can deliver," Ben snapped, then got a grip on himself. With less emotion, he added, "Your plan came into play after our original projections were scheduled for the year. I need to adjust fire, and it takes time."

Jamie was sure he was making excuses. They had worked out the scheduling together, and she knew he had already taken the change in marketing plans into consideration.

"If you need to redirect, let me know. We can work something out." Jamie suspected something else was bothering him but couldn't put her finger on it.

"How about you worry about your section, and I'll take care of mine?"

"How about working together for the good of the company?" She wasn't going to let this project fail because he couldn't manage his section.

"That's not what I meant," Ben amended.

Jamie crossed her arms and waited. Ben shuffled his feet, looking pathetic.

She let him struggle to come up with an excuse for being a jerk. After she felt he had suffered enough, Jamie backed off.

"When you're ready to discuss this like a professional, let me know." She started to walk away. "Oh," she added over her shoulder, "and Mom's doing better. Thanks for asking." The sarcasm was heavy in her words.

"What's wrong with your mom?" Ben asked, concerned.

Jamie stopped and turned back to him. "She got sick. That's why I had to go to Richmond," Jamie said. "Didn't Trina tell you?"

"No, she didn't."

Then it hit Jamie. "You thought I blew you off Friday night, didn't you?"

"No," Ben said defensively. "You didn't say for sure you were coming. But I was hoping to see you there." He looked down and shook his head, as if trying to shake something loose.

Jamie watched his internal struggle, and her mind raced. As the realization of his words hit her, her heart leapt. He cared enough to be mad at her for not showing up Friday night. Was she reading too much into it?

"I wish I could have been there," Jamie said, realizing how much she meant it. She watched his face. He was struggling with something, and she wished he would voice it.

"I'm sorry to hear about your mom, and I'm sorry I was a jerk." Ben hesitated then made up his mind. "I was looking forward to spending time with you away from work. I miss Colorado." There, he said it.

Jamie saw his face visibly change as the weight was lifted off his chest. She wasn't sure how to respond. She would love to spend more time with him and, she also missed Colorado. Telling him these things would not help their situation.

"I'm sorry I disappointed you," she said weakly. She wanted to promise to make it up to him but held her tongue. She was very close to crossing a line she didn't think she could recover from.

Ben looked into her eyes, and she was sure he could read her thoughts. "It's all for the best. I fared pretty well in the pool tournament. I didn't need the extra competition. You're probably a pool shark too."

"What do you mean 'too'?" Jamie asked, not denying the fact because she *was* a decent pool player.

"I saw you throw a football. There are many things I don't know about you yet. I'll bet you're full of surprises."

"Most definitely," Jamie said with a wink. "And some of them are even good."

Chapter 13

Ben's heart skipped a beat when he saw her down the hall. Jamie had her back to him, talking to the young kid from payroll. Ben ducked into the safety of his office suite.

"Sir, the reports you wanted will be here shortly. The printer is sending them over by courier," his secretary said.

Ben smiled and thanked her, stopping at her desk to filter through the messages stacked there for him. The door opened and closed. "Oh, good. I caught you."

At the sound of her voice, he closed his eyes and took a deep breath. Counting to three, he turned slowly to face her. "Jamie, I didn't realize you were chasing me," Ben said with a light-hearted laugh. "What's up?"

When she smiled back at him, he felt a tightening in his chest. *Why does she have such an effect on me?*

"I wanted to give you an update on some of the projects I've been working and get your thoughts."

"Come on in," he said, leading the way to his office. At the door, he stopped and let her go first. He watched her long legs up to her fitted skirt. No panty lines he could see. She took her customary seat in front of the desk, and Ben was tempted to touch her shoulder as he walked to his chair.

She was a lovely woman. Ben had never asked but gauged her age to be between thirty and thirty-five. Some men liked the idea of a younger woman, but Ben appreciated the sureness and maturity of someone with a little experience. They were more at ease in their own skin, and Jamie was a good example of confidence. She wore her chestnut hair below her shoulders in a casual style. She wore little to no make-up and only a thin chain around her neck.

He shifted in his seat as he glanced, subtly he hoped, at her cleavage. Pretty impressive. Not too showy but just enough to pique interest.

"Ben? Where are you today?" Jamie interrupted his musing. "You're not listening."

"I'm sorry. I'm a bit distracted. I've got a lot on my mind. What were you saying?"

As she left his office, Jamie couldn't help but smile. *Distracted? No shit,* she thought. *Maybe these new Victoria's Secret bras were worth the money after all.*

Her actions and attitudes recently were so out of character for her. She felt like she was back in high school again—and that wasn't necessarily a good thing. Her emotions were on a roller coaster. One minute she was happy and enjoying life; the next she was moody and sullen.

When she was at work, she could forget about Eddie and the other half of her life. The problem was, she had to go home. She *was* trying to make things work with Eddie, but he wasn't helping. He always had something else going on and somewhere else he needed to be. He rejected her advances, although she had to admit they were only half-hearted attempts.

They had been on shaky ground for a while. The difference was, Jamie no longer felt the strong need to make it right again. She had other things to keep her mind occupied.

Ben had such a power over her, and he didn't even know it. She thought of his thick, blond hair he had trouble keeping under control. His deep blue eyes twinkled when he smiled, which she had always thought was just an expression until she met him. She appreciated how he smiled often but could also be serious. What she found surprising was that it was such a turn-on to watch him work. His intellect was evident, but it was the way he expressed himself on so many topics which caught her attention. And he didn't talk down to people.

It was his ability to make everyone around him feel special which gave her pause. Was she special to him or was she just like everyone else?

The flirting was purely innocent, or at least that's what she told herself. A little flirting didn't hurt anyone. It was nice to have the attention, and it had been too long since she got it anywhere else. She knew she was appreciated as a businesswoman but sometimes a woman wants to be appreciated as a woman too—regardless of what the equal rights fanatics preached.

After Jamie left the office, Ben was kicking himself for being so unprofessional. He couldn't concentrate with her around and even now wasn't sure if he gave her the answers she needed. All he thought about was how he wanted to capture the magic he felt in Colorado Springs and have it play out every day, but he knew it wasn't realistic.

Now he was torn between finding an excuse to talk and avoiding her at all costs. He enjoyed her company but didn't like the power she held over him. He looked for her at every meeting but didn't sit by her if she did show up. Of course, then he was jealous of whomever she did sit by. *Dammit, it was like being in high school again,* he thought.

Jamie and Ben often met for lunch with others from the office. There was safety in numbers. At the very least, Trina could always be counted on to join them. Trina was still trying to capture Ben's attention, but as far as Jamie could tell, Ben didn't show her any extra interest. He flirted with her occasionally, but he flirted with all women in some way. Jamie was relieved he didn't single Trina out but couldn't explain why.

During one of their workday lunches, Trina went outside to take a phone call, leaving them alone. Ben picked up his water glass then set it down again. He started to pick it up again when Jamie started laughing. "What's wrong, Ben? You nervous to be alone with me?"

"Of course not." He took a drink. "I was just thinking you still owe me a drink."

"How do you figure?" she asked.

"I waited for you at the Tavern. I was so distraught; I drank at least one more gin and tonic than I had planned to."

"And that's my fault, how?"

"Well, had you shown up, I would have been in a better mood and wouldn't have had an extra drink. Therefore, you owe me," Ben finished as if he had really proven a point.

Jamie gave him credit for trying. "Sounds to me as though you already had the drink, so you're saying I owe you money for it."

Ben pretended to consider the merits of her argument. "Sounds logical. I say we discuss it further at dinner on Friday."

Jamie looked at the twinkle in his eye and could tell saying yes was inviting danger. Although the excitement the danger would bring was intriguing, she couldn't do it. She didn't think she was strong enough to be alone with him. She shifted uncomfortably in her seat. "I don't think it's such a good idea," she said.

Ben was clearly disappointed but not willing to give up. "We'll make it a quick drink then."

Jamie couldn't meet his eye. "Ben, I enjoy spending time with you," she said, picking up a paper napkin and tearing it into small pieces.

"Then this should be an easy decision," he said.

"I enjoy it too much," she went on. "You're dangerous for me."

Ben's thoughts hung on her phrase. "I take it you mean dangerous in a bad way."

"You know I'm married."

Jamie had finally said it. It was never a secret, but it wasn't something they talked about either. They talked about so much but left that piece of her life unexplored.

Ben reached across the table and tipped Jamie's chin up, so she looked into his eyes. Her sadness and conflict were reflected there.

"We can't do this," Jamie said. "We can only be friends."

"I know," Ben said. "That's all I want."

She searched his face and knew he was lying. She would be too.

Jamie shook her head and pushed her chair away from the table. Ben had to let her go.

Over the next few weeks, Jamie didn't exactly avoid Ben, but she didn't seek him out either. Her mind wandered to him often. She reenacted their conversations and their time together in Colorado Springs. She found herself thinking about him when she heard a funny joke and wanted to share it with him.

She saw couples walking with their arms around each other and envisioned being close to Ben. They were so natural and comfortable together; it was easier to picture them together than it was for her to picture Eddie holding her hand. She couldn't remember the last time she had gone out with her husband, let alone held hands.

She wondered how different things would be if she had met Ben years ago. She had been a different person back then. Would they still have hit it off? She liked to think so.

Chapter 14

Jamie found herself looking forward to First Fridays, as they came to be known. The first Friday of every month, a gang of people from work gathered at Liberty Tavern. Frequently it was the same crowd, but others would pop in on various occasions.

The Tavern was located on Wilson Boulevard amongst a host of other restaurants and bars in Arlington, Virginia. The green sign with white neon letters acted as a beacon calling to the after-work crowd. The red stone façade made the building one of the newer looking ones on the block.

A nice restaurant graced the upstairs with fifteen four-top tables, complete with white tablecloths and green napkins. The bar was on the ground floor with two pool tables, a dart board, booths against the wall, and high-top tables scattered throughout the room for people to lean on. The bar spanned half the length of the room and always had at least two bartenders on duty. They had a diverse wine list and got very creative with their specialty cocktails.

Trina was Jamie's steady date. Once in a while, Trina would bring a male friend, but they always included Jamie when buying rounds.

Jamie loved the camaraderie shared at these events. More and more she needed adult interaction. Eddie was rarely home. When he was, he wasn't interested in spending time with her. He said he needed his time to unwind.

Once again, the thought crept into her head that Eddie's interests were elsewhere, but she dismissed it. She had supposed it could be true but didn't want to face it. They had maintained a long-distance relationship for years before getting married, and he had never cheated. She passed this off as a phase every marriage goes through.

As Trina and Jamie walked from the parking garage to the Tavern, Trina's friend Tony greeted them. Although they'd been dating a few weeks now, Trina had confessed to Jamie that Tony wasn't a great kisser so she didn't think it would last.

Jamie couldn't help but think about the comment as Tony kissed Trina hello. Jamie stifled a grin as they entered the bar.

She surveyed the room. Most of the regulars were here but not many others. It was a beautiful weekend. Perhaps folks were trying to get a jump on their travel plans. Tony led them to a booth and squeezed in close to Trina, placing his arm around her shoulders. Jamie sat across from them and signaled for a waitress.

She ordered beers all around and considered what she was going to have for dinner. Eddie never made it home in time for dinner on Fridays, and First Friday had become as much of a routine for him as it had for Jamie. Trina and Tony were going out for a real dinner and had invited Jamie, but she wasn't going to interfere with their date.

The beer was delivered, and Jamie ordered appetizers. She was pleasantly surprised when Ben slid into the booth next to her, drink in hand. She felt his leg against hers and an electric current shot through her. She glanced at him to see if he had also felt it, but he was laughing at some comment Tony had made. He took a mouthful from his glass and gave her a sideways look she found hard to interpret.

She drank her own beer and lost herself in their company. When her food came, Ben helped himself. Jamie loved that their friendship was so comfortable. Several beers later, Tony and Trina excused themselves to make it in time for their dinner reservations. Once they left, it was an awkward moment when Jamie and Ben found themselves sitting side-by-side with no one to counterbalance the table.

"Guess I should move," Ben said.

"Probably would be best," Jamie said, although she relished the nearness of him.

Ben lingered a minute longer, struggling with what he wanted versus what was appropriate. With a sigh and a quick pat on her thigh, he repositioned himself on the other side of the table. "At least now it's easier to look at you."

Jamie blushed. She crossed her legs, and her foot brushed against him.

"Now don't start that again!" Ben complained.

"I didn't start it the first time," Jamie countered. But this was just the excuse she had been looking for to touch him. She let her foot make contact again, and Ben didn't pull away.

"I need another drink to cool down," Ben said, motioning for another round. Ben stared at Jamie, and she didn't avert her eyes. She had just enough alcohol in her to make her bold.

Another couple from work approached their table and asked if they could join them.

Jamie was disappointed when Ben jumped up and welcomed them. Then he excused himself to go to the restroom. When he returned, the couple had taken his place in the booth, leaving the seat next to Jamie open. This time when he took his seat, Jamie didn't allow as much room for him. She reminded herself of the dangers of this game, then a picture of Eddie hanging with his dart buddies instead of her flashed through her head. She decided to allow herself a good time.

Usually by this time in the evening, Jamie would have been circulating among her other friends, but she didn't want to give up this opportunity for physical contact with Ben. Ben didn't seem in a hurry to move either and had even passed up a challenge at the pool table. Jamie knew it wouldn't last long. People were starting to clear out, shouting goodbyes as they passed the table.

When the couple across from them decided to call it a night, Jamie said it was time for her to go too. She wasn't sure she could stand having Ben move away from her again—being so close but not able to touch him. They all stood together, and Ben offered to walk Jamie to her car. Jamie agreed.

The noise of the passing motorists were quiet compared to the din inside the bar. The streetlights were on, casting a pleasant glow on the few pedestrians meandering by.

As they walked the few blocks to the parking garage, they didn't talk. It was a relaxed silence, and Jamie was very happy. The fresh air was sobering her up which was good and bad. She felt guilty for flirting so outright, but it made her feel sensual. Ben made her feel desirable and important— something she hadn't felt in a long time.

Jamie thought about how good it would feel to take his hand as they walked. It would be the most natural thing in the world under other circumstances.

Ben waited for Jamie to get in her car and start it before waving and walking away. His car was up another level, so he headed for the stairs.

Jamie watched him go, already missing the nearness of him. She opened her phone. A text message from Eddie,

"Will be very late. Don't wait up." Typical, she thought as she snapped it closed. Another lonely night.

Chapter 15

The dim room was lit by strings of bare white bulbs hanging from the ceiling. The stonework on the walls was realistic and gave the restaurant a cozy, Italian feel. The wine glasses were stacked in towers on buffet tables in the middle of the room, inviting with the light twinkling off them. It was too noisy to be romantic, but Jamie felt the excitement building in her as the hostess seated them.

She was quiet and embarrassed when Ben insisted on pulling her chair out.

The offer for an after-work drink had turned into a dinner invitation when Ben discovered Jamie would be dining alone again. At first Jamie had said no, but then a hint of defiance made her change her mind. Eddie made business dinner plans without consulting her. She hadn't been out to eat in ages. It was her turn.

Now sitting in the restaurant looking across the table at Ben, Jamie got nervous. What was she getting herself into? She accepted his suggestion of a glass of Merlot when the waiter came back to take their drink order.

"Did your brother-in-law get the job he interviewed for?" Jamie asked while she looked over the menu.

"He got called back for a second interview," Ben responded. He closed the menu and put it aside. "He's hopeful."

Jamie loved that Ben was close with his family. Never having had siblings, she was envious of their interaction and enjoyed the stories. Throughout dinner, Ben told Jamie of the mean tricks they played on each other growing up, and Jamie laughed at the creative punishments his mother came up with. She could listen to him forever.

"So, how did you meet Eddie?" Ben asked.

Jamie was taken aback by the question. This was new territory for them. She took a drink of water and thought about where to start. Staring into the twinkling wine glasses, she recited her story without emotion.

"We met the summer break between our junior and senior years in college. I was home for the summer, and he was visiting his parents who had just moved to town. Our dads met at the golf course and somehow managed to introduce us. We went out pretty much every night for the next four weeks. Eddie was fun to be around. He was always joking." She took another drink of water. Ben could hear something else in her voice but didn't press her on the subject.

"He went back to Penn State; I went back to William and Mary. We dated long distance for our senior year. Then Eddie started law school. He spent most his time studying, but we were still officially dating. I had started work at SAE, so I was busy too. We'd see each other one weekend a month, give or take." She stopped.

"And?" Ben prompted when it didn't look like she was going to resume.

Jamie shrugged. "It just kind of happened. When he graduated law school, we had already been dating for so long everyone assumed we'd get married. Our dads were practically counting on it. One weekend, Eddie took me to the jewelry store, and we picked out rings." She shrugged again.

"That's it?" Ben was truly surprised. "No fancy dinner, ring hidden in the dessert?" He tried to make her smile. She was subdued after the tale.

"Eddie was never the romantic."

"And now?" Ben asked.

"I think all those years we dated apart set his expectations for something very different in a marriage. I'm not sure he knows how to share his life with someone. He still works all the time. His hours are crazy." Jamie played with her napkin. "What about you? Why haven't you ever been married?" she said, redirecting the spotlight.

"I'm waiting for the right person."

"Have you ever been close?"

"When I was only thinking with my head and not my heart, I considered it once. Susan and I had been dating a long time, and she was fun to be around. She hinted enough for a ring, but I wasn't feeling it. Part of me felt guilty; like I had been stringing her along, but it wasn't intentional. I almost gave in with a what-the-heck attitude."

"What stopped you?"

"My sisters. I mentioned Susan and I getting married to Candi, my youngest sister. She was totally against it. She said she didn't think we were a good match. She couldn't give me any hard examples of why. Before I had gotten back to my apartment that night, my other two sisters had called to dissuade me. I figured they were seeing something I wasn't, so I broke it off with her."

"Bet she was mad."

Ben shrugged. "Mostly because I didn't give her a reason, I think. I certainly wasn't going to say, 'because my sisters don't want me to marry you.' As far as she knew, everything was going fine, then the next day we broke up."

They lapsed into a comfortable silence. They were one of the few couples still left in the restaurant. Ben played with the extra silverware on the table, spinning the fork against the table.

Jamie swirled the wine in her glass. She had stopped drinking at least an hour before, knowing she still had to drive home. She liked the way the sugar from the red wine made icicles down the inside of the glass. When she looked up, Ben was gazing at her. "Where's my quarter when I need it?" he asked.

"Those thoughts were worth a lot more than a quarter."

"In that case…" Ben pulled out a twenty-dollar bill and placed it on the table. "I definitely want to hear it."

Jamie blushed. She knew some thoughts she could never share with anyone—even Ben.

Ben watched Jamie turn red and could only hope he was right in what she was thinking. He thought about it way too much but certainly wouldn't be the first one to admit it. He wasn't trying to pressure her in any way but couldn't deny his feelings. When he thought of Eddie, his anger grew, not simply out of jealousy, although that was part of it. More so because Jamie deserved to be treated better. Her so-called husband didn't warrant this exceptional woman, and Ben was afraid the bad marriage would break her.

He watched her smile, and his heart melted. Jamie was fun and easy to talk to. She listened and cared about what he said, never told him he needed to grow up or he should think a different way.

They flirted a lot, but they had kept their boundaries intact. They had a good thing going, and he wasn't about to cross the line. Although when she laid her hand on his arm while sharing a secret, it was all he could do to keep from closing his hand over hers to hold her in place. He envisioned wrapping her in his arms and kissing her; he spent enough time staring at her lips.

Dammit! What would my sisters think? Ben chastised himself, trying to logic his way back to the surface. They would not condone him chasing after a married woman, no matter her circumstances.

But they sure would like Jamie.

She slammed the car door and banged her head against the steering wheel. *Why do I keep doing this to myself?* She fought back the tears, knowing once they started, she'd have a hard time stopping them. Taking deep breaths, she focused on the warmth inside the car, allowing it to seep into her bones.

She loved the excitement, the challenge, and the thrill she got from her interactions with Ben. But she knew she was playing with fire. She was married, and it couldn't go anywhere. She'd never get to feel Ben's arms around her, wake up beside him, feel his touch, his mouth. *Dammit!* She was doing it again.

She knew the right thing to do was to stay away from him. Don't talk to him, don't text him, don't answer the phone if he calls. But the draw was so powerful. He made her happy. Ben could make her feel good about herself with a single look or smile. Jamie smiled to herself thinking about their conversation at the coffee bar that morning. They always talked around the subject of their attraction but never faced it directly; it would be too painful. When he offered to get her coffee, she had asked, "Think you can handle it?" She was referring to the coffee order, of course, but everything can be taken two ways.

His response still shot a spark of electricity through her as she thought of it. "I know I can." The intensity in his eyes left no doubt what he was referring to although it wasn't verbalized. It didn't have to be.

One more deep breath and Jamie started the car. She had to go home to her husband.

Chapter 16

The next day went by in a frustrating blur. Jamie rode the roller coaster of exhilaration when she thought of the wonderful evening she had spent with Ben. The low points were when thoughts of Eddie crept into her subconscious. The notion of preferring the company of another man over her husband pushed aside any sense of well-being she had built up. The weight of the guilt was oppressive, and she had to pull herself out of the hopelessness to interact with people at work.

She made up her mind to stop dwelling on what wasn't and to concentrate on improving what she had. As she shut down her computer for the evening, she turned her thoughts toward the things she had to be thankful for. She had her health, a good job, good friends, a great mother and stepfather. She had a roof over her head and food on the table. Her husband may not love her but at least he didn't beat her. She could live with that…she supposed.

There were no lights on in the windows as she pulled up, but she wasn't surprised. She paused outside the small house, regarding it with new eyes. It was a white, two-story with blue shutters and only a front stoop, not a porch. The flat front, uniform on the left and right, was not her style. She would prefer something with its own personality, a little offset. The house was in a nice neighborhood, but they didn't socialize with their neighbors much. The garden outside needed some work but it wasn't bad. Jamie took in the whole picture. The word "boring" flashed in her mind.

She was never taken with the house. Eddie and his dad had purchased it when Jamie was still in college. After their marriage, she followed the plan and moved in. She was able to add a little of her character through decorating ideas, but Eddie was very picky, so she wasn't able to change much.

When she walked in the door, the house was quiet. With a sigh of relief, she dropped her purse on the granite counter and went to hang her sweater in the hall closet.

Opening the door, she could smell her husband's aftershave permeating from his favorite sports coat. She ran her hand over the rough fabric of the tweed. The faint scratchy feeling as she pulled the sleeve to her face brought back fond memories. Now she did cry.

She cried for the times past. For the time when Eddie was the one who made her tingle all over, even if it was only once a month. It had been years, but Jamie knew there was once a time when he did care about her. She prayed it would be like that again. She didn't want to give up on her promise of forever. She believed their marriage could be saved, but every day that slipped by carried the possibility further out of reach.

She heard the garage door open. Eddie was home. She closed the closet door and headed for the kitchen.

"Hi, honey," she said as he walked through the door. She stepped forward to kiss him, but he sidestepped her and headed for the living room, mumbling something as he passed.

She froze in place, willing herself to overlook the slight yet again. No matter how hard she tried, she wasn't able to reach him. How much longer would she be willing to try?

She shook off the melancholy and turned her mind toward dinner. She poured herself a glass of wine to sip as she pulled dishes from the cupboards.

She remembered picking out these dishes. Eddie wasn't interested, so Jamie and her mother had spent the day shopping. They went from store to store, taking notes and revisiting some stores multiple times before deciding on the white plates with small hearts around the rim. They were simple, which suited Jamie, but had a touch of color to make her smile.

For dinner, she made a simple dish of chicken parmesan with spaghetti. Early in their marriage, they joked that chicken was the only meat she could cook. She rarely made anything else. Spaghetti was Eddie's specialty.

When he joined her at the table, Jamie tried to tell him about Trina and her latest boyfriend. He wasn't listening, so she stopped talking mid-sentence. He didn't notice.

Dejected, she got up to serve the coffee and apple pie—his favorite. She slid back into her seat and picked up her fork. Eddie ran his hand absently across his mouth and then up to his ear. How many times had she seen him do that? She knew all his habits; it came with years of being together. She wondered if he noticed those things in her. She took a bite of pie.

Eddie cleared his throat but didn't speak.

"What's on your mind?" Jamie asked. He didn't look at her.

"Nothing you would understand," he replied dismissively.

"Maybe you should try me."

Eddie snorted. She cringed.

He took another bite of his pie and pushed the plate away. "I'm going to bed." He got up and walked out of the kitchen, leaving half his dessert untouched, and his dishes on the table.

Jamie sat brooding. Then she got up, cleared the table, and threw his pie in the trash—plate and all.

Chapter 17

That night, Jamie tossed and turned as thoughts of Ben filled her dreams. She awoke upon climax as Ben penetrated all her defenses and her body in the most satisfying sex she had had in years—and it was all a dream. Jamie threw the covers off to cool her sweating body. Eddie snored next to her. She probably could have sex with another man right under his nose, and he wouldn't notice. He didn't pay attention to anything she did.

As Jamie replayed the dream in her head, excitement stirred in her again. She and Ben were walking along the beach when they came to an alcove. There was a cave and Ben tried to pull her in, but she was afraid. He put his arms around her and kissed her throat. She gave in. They walked arm in arm into the damp, dark space. Ben pulled a blanket from somewhere and spread it on the ground. She didn't remember him carrying it, but it was a dream, after all.

They kissed again, long, slow, and deep. Ben's hands played down her body, lingering on her breasts.

In her bed, Jamie allowed her hands to follow the path Ben's took in her dream.

He never stopped kissing her as he unbuttoned her top and slid it over her shoulders. In her dream, Ben bent to kiss the tops of her breasts, whispering something Jamie couldn't quite hear. She ran her fingers through his hair and pulled his head closer to her. His hands reached behind her and unhooked the black lacy bra she was wearing. Now his tongue touched her right nipple, making it harder than it already was.

Jamie felt under her nightgown and touched her breasts. Her nipples were hard.

In her dream, Ben's right hand caressed her left breast, cupping it softly. Now he switched sides and took her left breast into his mouth, sucking gently while never neglecting her right side. Jamie moaned and her knees were weak. Ben pulled back and kissed her mouth while lowering her to the blanket.

Ben was bare chested now although Jamie didn't know how that happened. She pulled him down to her and could feel his hardness against her groin. She pushed against him, wanting to feel him, needing to feel him. He pushed her short skirt up and ran his hand along the inside of her thigh. She was so excited, she was breathless.

Jamie reached between her legs and the wetness was silky soft.

Jamie reached for dream-Ben. He was long and hard in her hand. He moaned as she slipped his shorts and boxers over his hips, releasing his shaft from its captivity. She worked her hand up and down its length, dying to feel him inside of her. She had waited so long for this moment. His fingers deftly worked their way between her folds, spreading the wetness over her, massaging tenderly. As she stroked him, she felt the drops of natural lubrication and ran her thumb over the tip of his shaft. He climbed on top of her, and she guided him to her, rubbing his tip against her clitoris.

The cave suddenly grew brighter, and Jamie saw tables set up around them. There were people sitting at the tables drinking. Ben didn't notice. Jamie froze. Ben pushed himself against her, opening her with his bulk. Jamie was so excited, but she didn't want people watching. She didn't know what to do. Ben kissed her again and the people clapped.

"They don't matter," Ben whispered as he pushed harder against her. Jamie relaxed her thighs and welcomed him in, sighing as his hardness filled her. She closed her eyes but could hear the murmurs coming from the tables. Ben thrust deeper but it wasn't hard enough. Jamie raised her hips to meet him.

Jamie got up from the bed and went into the guest room, locking the door behind her. She stripped off her nightgown and soaked panties. She laid back on the cool bed and spread her legs. Her fingers slid over her mound, and she felt the heat. Then she returned to her dream.

Ben kissed her neck and stroked her with his fingers as he moved inside her. Harder and harder. But it wasn't hard enough for Jamie. She rocked her hips to meet him and take him in deeper. In her dream and on the guest room bed, Jamie came with an explosion for the second time that night.

As she lay on the bed sweating, the guilt overtook her again. She couldn't control her dreams, but she shouldn't have continued the fantasy while awake. *But damn!* A satisfied smile appeared on her face. She wondered if Ben could live up to the dream-Ben.

Now that the arousal was dissipating, she took time to wonder about the other people in her dream. Who were they and why were they watching? How could she have sex with people watching? She wondered what it said about her.

But, in the end, it was a dream and dreams didn't have to make sense. As the sweat cooled on her body, she started to feel chilled. She slid her nightgown back on and picked up her panties. Slipping back into her room, she dropped them in the hamper and crawled back in bed. At least she would sleep well the rest of the night.

The next day at work, Jamie flushed when she saw Ben in the hall talking with Trina. He waved at her, but she ducked into the ladies' room before he got too close. She felt hot remembering the dream and ran cool water in the sink.

When she left the restroom, the hall was clear. Jamie walked to her office, stopping to visit with Carolyn and pick up messages. She made her way to her desk, sifting through the stack of papers her secretary had handed her.

"Are you up for lunch?" She jumped at the sound of Ben's voice. "Sorry, didn't mean to startle you," Ben said. "A group of us are going to Thai Basil for lunch. Want to go?"

Jamie couldn't look directly at Ben without picturing him naked on top of her. "I better pass today. I've got a lot going on. Thanks for the offer though."

"Okay. Next time." Ben departed as quickly as he had entered her office.

She had to get Ben out of her mind and focus on her husband. She pulled out her phone and sent Eddie a text. "Need u home on time 2nite."

Jamie left work a little early to ensure she had time for her preparations. She took a quick shower, shaved, and put lotion on her legs. She searched through her dresser until she found the white lingerie she had worn on their honeymoon. She set candles on the bedside tables and lit them. The stereo was in the living room but was piped throughout the house via the sound system. Jamie picked out music from their dating days.

Jamie was nervous. She felt a little silly walking through her house wearing so little, but at the same time, a little sexy too. She slipped into the kitchen and opened a bottle of chilled white wine. She pulled two glasses from the china cabinet they only used on special occasions and poured herself a drink.

While she waited for Eddie to get home, she tried to steel herself against the rejection. She would not take no for an answer this time. As she sipped her second glass, sitting on the couch in her silk, she played the scenario through her mind.

She imagined answering the door to a stranger by accident. She blushed at the thought but felt herself getting aroused all the same. The wine was relaxing her and making her braver.

She heard the garage door open and close, then the door to the house. She stood and took a deep breath. Eddie walked in and tossed his keys on the kitchen table. He stripped off his coat and hung it in the coat closet. He still hadn't noticed her.

He stepped toward the living room and halted when he caught sight of Jamie. Only then did the music and the low lights register in his brain. Jamie saw him sigh.

"Jamie, it's been a long day," he started.

She refused to let his attitude discourage her. She set her wine glass on the coffee table and approached him. She tried not to rush and to walk like she thought a sexy woman should walk. His head was down, and his hands were on his hips.

She slid her hands up his chest and around his neck, kissing his ear. His hands remained at his side. She rubbed her body against him and tried to ignore the burning embarrassment she felt at his non-reaction.

Her hands worked their way down his arms until his hands were in hers. She slowly and deliberately raised them until his hands covered her breasts. She tried to look him in the face, but he wouldn't raise his eyes.

His hands stayed motionless against her breasts. She couldn't take it anymore. Jamie pushed him hard in the chest, causing him to stumble back a few steps. Then she slapped him across the face and ran from the room.

Slamming the bedroom door closed, she leaned against it crying. From the living room, she heard him at the bar mixing himself a drink.

Chapter 18

The next day, Eddie was making no excuses to avoid a sexual encounter. This is what he had been waiting for and fantasizing about.

He watched as she entered the bedroom, dressed in red and black. Very little material covered her perfect form. The heels she wore left marks in the carpeting as she approached the bed.

This would never happen in his monotonous daily life. He couldn't imagine Jamie being willing to even *try* something so out of the ordinary. The fact that he was bringing another woman to their bed made the transgression even more exciting.

He had taken women to hotel rooms while on business trips, done it in the back seat of their cars, but had never brought one home. He was getting more and more daring.

Next time he crawled into bed beside Jamie, he would be thinking about the woman in black lace. It might even be sufficient to spark enough interest for him to give Jamie some of what she had been begging for lately.

Bodies slick with sweat, he pushed them into a sitting position. She laughed as he licked the droplets off first one breast then the other. She wrapped her legs around his waist and rotated her hips. He growled under his breath as he tried to control his reaction.

She nibbled at his ear and entwined her fingers in his hair. Suddenly she jerked his head back in a violent motion. The flash of fear in his eyes swiftly turned to passion as she forcefully ground her body against him. He tried to lean in to kiss her, and she struck him painfully across the face. A trickle of blood slid out the corner of his mouth.

He begged with his eyes to get closer to her.

She rose to her feet until she was standing over him on the bed. His hands found the back of her thighs and slid up to her buttocks.

In one swift motion, she stepped back, placed a foot on the center of his chest, and shoved him brutally back on the bed. His arms collapsed under him. Leading with her knees to his chest, she let her full body weight fall unhindered on top of him, without giving him time to brace himself. The air was forced from his lungs, and he gasped. She laughed and lowered her body to cover his face.

As he struggled, she moved her hips over his face, ignoring his hands trying to push her away so he could catch his breath.

At lunchtime, Jamie decided to take off for the rest of the day. Her situation with Eddie was bothering her, and she couldn't focus. Having Ben nearby didn't help. She wanted to make things work with Eddie, but she couldn't do anything right. They needed to talk.

She wanted to love Eddie like she used to, but she felt nothing for him—not love but not hate either. She would try one more time. Maybe make his favorite meal. Jamie ran through a shopping list in her mind as she parked in the driveway. She'd be going out again soon, so she didn't bother with the garage. She unlocked the front door and left her keys on the hall table.

She needed to change her clothes before going shopping. Taking the stairs two steps at a time, she felt more confident in her resolve. She slowed when she noticed the bedroom door was closed. They always left it open for air circulation.

Jamie approached quietly and could hear muffled sounds on the other side of the door. Fear coursed through her. Then, as she stood frozen, her fear changed to a deeper, darker emotion—rage.

Jamie flung the door open, the knob smashing an indent in the wall.

The woman turned toward the sound but didn't stop her grinding. She grinned at Jamie. The man underneath her used the distraction to get his purchase and pushed her aside. He sat up gasping for air and coughing. The woman laughed and lay back on the bed. She didn't bother trying to cover up.

Jamie took in the scene with disgust. The woman was young with a beautiful figure, but she was marked with various tattoos and piercings. A snake figure curled around her neck and across her breast, its open mouth with fangs ready to pierce her right nipple. Her eyes were outlined with thick black makeup and her dark hair was teased to an unnatural rat's nest.

Eddie looked pathetic, red from coughing and naked except the black lace panties he was wearing over his groin. He looked up at Jamie, and his face turned a darker shade of crimson.

Jamie couldn't take it any longer. She fled from the room, stumbling into the hall bathroom and falling to her knees in front of the toilet. She heaved uncontrollably until there was nothing left. As she waited for the next wave to come, she heard a sound behind her. She didn't bother to turn. The clicking footsteps stopped outside her door, and Jamie heard a quiet, feminine chuckle. Then the steps resumed. Moments later the front door opened and closed.

She slumped to the floor and let the tile cool her fevered face.

She sensed a presence in the doorway. Without bothering to sit up, she mustered enough energy to mutter, "Get out," and slammed the door closed with her foot.

After lying on the floor long enough for the sun to set and the room to turn dark, Jamie stood. She made her way back down to the kitchen on weak legs and rummaged through the cupboard. Finally, she found what she was looking for. She poured a tall shot of tequila into a glass and downed it in one gulp.

Ben exited the metro near the bar Jamie had summoned him to and walked the short distance. It was a quiet night, and he heard the music before he opened the door. The cool air greeted him, and he peered into the darkness looking for her. She was sitting alone in a booth in the back corner.

"What's going on, Jamie?" Ben asked as he slid into the red, plastic booth across from her.

She smiled a crooked smile at him. "This is your rain-check. You okay with that?"

Ben grinned back. "Of course. Bit unexpected but I'll take it." Ben looked at her attentively. "How long have you been here?"

Jamie's eyes were unfocused as she looked back at him. "Not too long," she answered.

Ben laughed. "Okay, if you say so."

The waitress approached him, and he ordered some food for them. Jamie ordered a beer, but Ben changed the order to water.

Jamie threw a bar napkin at him but didn't argue. While they waited, they made small talk about people at work.

When the food came, she dug in. Ben watched and made sure she was sobering up as the food absorbed some of the alcohol in her system. This time when she ordered a beer, Ben let her.

They talked until very late, exchanging stories. Ben focused on getting Jamie to forget whatever it was that had brought her to this bar in a blue mood. She finally relaxed and began laughing with him. When she covered her mouth with her hand to hide her teeth, Ben reached forward and pulled her hand down.

"Why do you do that?" he asked.

"Do what?"

"Cover your smile. It's beautiful. I love when you laugh."

Jamie gazed at him, very appreciative for his kindness. "I wore braces when I was younger. I guess old habits die hard," she explained.

"Some habits are worth breaking," Ben said as he released her hand and reached for his drink.

When the bartender called for last rounds, Ben was surprised how the time had passed. He was disappointed their night was over.

"Going to walk me home?" Jamie asked with a mischievous glint in her eye.

"Of course. Don't want you to take advantage of some poor unsuspecting stranger on your way home."

"But I can take advantage of you?" Jamie stared at Ben intently.

"We'll see," Ben countered, feeling the stirrings he had been trying to suppress all night.

He stood and held out a hand to help Jamie from her seat. She held it a little longer than necessary, but Ben wasn't about to complain. When he was sure she was steady enough to walk, Ben led the way to the door and held it open for her. Then he enjoyed the view as he watched her head down the sidewalk in front of him toward the metro.

During the walk, Jamie took Ben's arm. The heat she was radiating was more than he thought he could stand. She laughed and told stories about her imaginary childhood friend. She talked nonstop through the metro trip and to her car in the metro parking lot, but never mentioned the reason she ended up at the bar that night.

She fished out her keys and handed them to Ben. He took them without question and unlocked the passenger door. He helped her into the car. As he walked around to get in the driver's side, he took a deep breath and willed himself to stay in control. She was definitely tempting.

A short drive later, Jamie hit the button to open the garage door, and he pulled the car in. Ben noted the empty spot in the next stall over and was relieved he wasn't going to meet Jamie's husband under these circumstances. She jumped out and headed for the door.

"I better get going," Ben said.

Jamie laughed at him, still a bit tipsy. "Eddie's not coming home." She came back and grabbed his hand, pulling him toward the house.

Ben followed her, unsure what he should do next.

"Shit," she muttered as she fumbled for the light switch. With a click, light illuminated the pale cabinets and dark granite countertops.

Jamie pulled out two wine glasses and poured from a bottle of red wine sitting open on the table. Ben noted the empty tequila bottle on the counter. With a flourish, she offered Ben a glass. He accepted the wine, but Jamie didn't release it right away. She locked eyes with him, drawing him closer.

Ben broke eye contact first. He took the glass from her hand and walked across the room. "This is a nice house," he said.

Jamie took a long drink and looked around as if for the first time. "It's boring," she replied. "Did Trina tell you about Kevin's latest stunt at work?" Jamie changed the subject as she led him into the living room and settled on the couch, pulling him down beside her.

She sat at an angle, with her bent leg on the couch touching his thigh. He rested his arm on the back of the couch and tried to follow her story.

Ben loved listening to Jamie. She was captivating, even more so when she had been drinking and wasn't so self-conscious. Her suggestive comments were having an unnerving effect on him though. It was taking every ounce of his self-control to not take advantage of being truly alone with her.

"Ben, you aren't listening again," Jamie said.

"Sorry," Ben said.

"It's okay. I know you were thinking about kissing me," Jamie said matter-of-factly.

Dammit, she's killing me, Ben thought. Audibly he asked, "How would you know what I was thinking?"

"Because you've been thinking about it for months now." Jamie's winning smile was so inviting. She leaned forward conspiratorially. "I like how you think."

Ben watched her lips but didn't admit he had thought about a lot more than kissing her.

Jamie rested back on the couch, open to whatever would happen next. "You should kiss me now."

Ben's will was breaking. She was beautiful and unbelievably desirable. He approached her slowly, giving her a chance to change her mind. Her eyes were shining, and her lips were moist. *Dammit*, he thought again as he felt himself giving in. He placed his hands on either side of her head and lowered himself close to her.

Jamie seemed to be holding her breath, and Ben wondered if she regretted her challenge. He watched Jamie's lovely face as he drew closer. He wanted her so much but once he started, he didn't know if he could stop. He had imagined this very moment many times. His lips brushed her forehead, and he felt Jamie shudder. He worked his way down to her neck, barely touching her skin. Jamie opened her eyes and reached for him, but Ben held himself, not putting any weight on her.

Ben looked into Jamie's wanting eyes and felt his resolve caving. He pushed himself into a standing position. "Not tonight," Ben said huskily. It took all his effort to turn and walk away. He left Jamie reclining on the couch as he closed the door behind him.

Ben was trembling as he walked down the street. A cool breeze dried the sweat on his face and neck. He had planned on grabbing a cab after dropping Jamie off, but now he was grateful for the chance to walk off his sexual frustrations.

"What kind of game is she playing?" he said aloud to the night sky. He kicked a stone and heard it clatter on the pavement. A small animal darted in front of him and into the shadows of the bushes lining the neighboring yards.

Ben picked up his pace. He couldn't shake the image of her so vulnerable before him—mentally as well as physically. He wanted for nothing more than to take away her pain, but he knew one night of sexual release wouldn't be the right answer. Ben needed to focus on her long-term happiness, not just this one night. He didn't know what was going on in her life, but she wasn't acting like herself.

He reached the metro station and headed home. He stared out the window and watched the blur of lights, thinking about how things might have gone differently. Those thoughts only succeeded in renewing the hard-on Jamie had so aptly started. By the time he got to his house, he was pulsing.

He didn't bother turning on the lights as he went straight to his room and began undressing with the intent of calming himself in a very cold shower.

He ran the water and tested it briefly before stepping in. The shock of ice on his skin awoke his senses but did little to deflate the erection desperately needing attention.

Turning off the water, he reached for a towel. A little shaky, he dried his arms and then his legs. He had a strange feeling in the pit of his stomach he couldn't quite put his finger on.

Guilt. That was it. But what did he have to be guilty about? He struggled with himself as he tried to reason through his mood. His feelings for Jamie were so intense he didn't want to cheapen them with fantasies that could never be real.

He wrapped the towel around his waist and grabbed a dry towel from the rack to run over his hair. He moved into the bedroom and dropped backwards on the bed, covering his face with the towel.

He needed to move on.

Chapter 19

Saturday Jamie spent most of the morning in bed. She was marginally hung over but, more than that, she was miserable about her situation. Her husband had been sleeping around, but she wasn't even capable of seducing the one man who had shown her the most interest in years.

Whenever she replayed the evening in her head, she felt a wave of shame and embarrassment. Ben must think she was such a pathetic fool.

At the time, tequila seemed like the right answer to drown her sorrows. Now, as she tried to piece together the mess of the night before, she wasn't so sure.

She was surprised Ben had actually come out to meet her on such short notice. And he had looked good too. He was dressed in jeans tight enough to accentuate his thighs but not too tight. His short-sleeved t-shirt hugged his chest and showed off his muscular arms.

She had been so nervous she felt like a teenager about to lose her virginity.

Then he was gone. She wasn't sure what she had done wrong, but she scared him away.

Eventually the tears came. Jamie cried for her stupidity, for her failed marriage, and for her unknown future.

When she had no tears left, Jamie forced herself out of bed. After gulping down a large glass of cold water, she filled her glass again and took it to the kitchen table, sitting down heavily. She rested her forehead on the table and replayed the night before. Try as she might, she couldn't undo any of her actions, or even think of a way to explain them away next time she saw Ben. She was at a loss as to what to do.

By noon she was finished feeling sorry for herself. *Eddie is such a shit*, she thought, not for the first time. She was going to get up and go for a run. No matter that she hadn't gone jogging in years; she needed to start a new routine, and this was right time. Anything to occupy her mind.

Ben didn't sleep at all that night. He kept seeing Jamie vulnerable under him on the couch. He wanted her so much but didn't want her desire to be alcohol induced. Ben would take her, married or not, but he didn't want her to regret it afterward. He wouldn't be able to live with himself if he hurt her.

As he washed dishes that had been piling up over the past week, he thought about past women in his life. He had only spent any amount of time with one—Susan. She was nice and Ben liked her, but she wasn't the one he was waiting for. They only stayed together as long as they had because he enjoyed her company.

It wasn't until he realized she was getting serious that he decided to call it quits. He didn't want to string her along. He did miss her for a while after they broke up, but more like a friend than a lover. Following Susan, Ben was a lot more selective in whom he dated. He preferred going out with groups of friends rather than dates.

Until Jamie.

He would prefer to be alone with her for any reason but felt there was safety in numbers. He was forced to control himself with others watching and chaperoning them.

Ben dried his hands and looked around for his next project. For the rest of the weekend, he worked hard around the house. He caught up on small projects he had been meaning to do—anything to stop thinking about Jamie. He was dreading Monday morning.

Jamie was late getting to work on Monday. Nothing was going right. She couldn't find the matching jacket for her skirt, she had misplaced her car keys, and she got stuck behind an accident on the highway.

This is one way to avoid Ben, she thought.

When she pulled into her spot, the lot was full. She had called Carolyn on the way in to warn her she'd be late and to send someone else to the Monday staff meeting. Jamie was able to slip into her office without seeing anyone but her secretary. She closed the door behind her and dove into the paperwork on her desk.

A little before lunch, Carolyn stuck her head in the office. "Mr. Hardy's secretary called. Mr. Hardy would like to see you when you have a minute."

"Did he say what it's about?"

"No," Carolyn said. "I asked but his secretary didn't know."

It wasn't unusual for Steven to call for her, but she was used to having a heads up so she could prepare in advance. This time she didn't have a clue, so she gathered her notes on her latest projects.

She was ushered into his office and took the seat in front of his desk, declining his offer of coffee.

"Jamie, I have a favor to ask," Steven started. Steven Hardy was a kind man in his late fifties. His dark features and quick smile were a topic of conversation around the office. The slight graying at the temples gave him a very distinguished look. Jamie suspected there were many young ladies with a crush on him, but he remained devoted to his wife of forty years.

"Anything." Jamie respected Steven very much and was more than willing to help him out if she could.

"The Virginia Beach office needs some help. Some of the staff have filed complaints against senior management there, but I don't think we have the whole story. I need someone I can trust to be my eyes and ears."

Jamie listened intently as Steven outlined the complaint and what actions had been taken so far. When he finished, he asked, "I know it's a lot to ask, but would you be willing to go to Virginia Beach for a few months and look things over?"

Jamie thought over the projects she had and hesitated. Then she thought about Ben and Eddie. "Of course I'll go," she replied. This couldn't have come at a better time for her. She needed some distance.

Steven added more detail and handed her a file containing the complaints. "We'll give you as much time as you need, but I would prefer if you could go right away. Will it be a problem? Do you want to check with your husband?"

"Not a problem. Let me tie up some loose ends today, and I can probably leave tomorrow afternoon." Jamie stood and tapped the file. "This could be messy."

"I know it won't be easy, but I'm sure you can sort it out. We'll put you up at the Westin while you're down there."

Jamie nodded and headed for the door. "I'll give you an update as soon as I get a chance to dig into it a bit."

When Jamie sat down behind her computer again, she had mixed feelings—relieved to be getting away from Ben but missing him already. As an afterthought, she thought of Eddie. This timing would work out well after all.

Chapter 20

Jamie spent the afternoon typing up notes on unfinished projects so her assistant could pick up where she left off. She was tied up in her office until late trying to get things organized. When she left, the parking lot was empty.

Eddie's car was parked in the garage when she pulled in. Jamie steeled herself against the conversation to come. She entered the kitchen and placed her purse on the counter. She made her way through the house to the bedroom. There was a suitcase on the bed, half-full of Eddie's clothes.

Eddie came out of the bathroom with his shaving kit. He paused when he saw her, but then continued packing. "I contacted the lawyer today," he said. "He'll be sending you paperwork to review. I'd rather not have to go to court over this."

Jamie knew she told him to leave and not come back, but this seemed so fast. She just nodded. Eddie continued moving about the room.

"Can you at least tell me why?" she managed to ask.

Eddie sat on the edge of the bed and looked everywhere but at Jamie. He thought for a minute before answering. "I didn't plan it."

"But you didn't stop it either," Jamie said curtly. She softened her voice. "You could have come to me. We could have talked about it, gone to counseling or something."

"I don't need counseling," Eddie said.

"Right. Because seeking help would imply you could improve and that isn't possibly an option for you, is it?" Jamie said, crossing her arms across her chest.

"Why would I pay money to talk about feelings and point fingers? We could just talk it out on our own."

"But we didn't, did we? You never wanted to talk. And now it's too late," Jamie said.

Eddie got up and continued packing without another word.

Jamie left the room and went back to the kitchen. She wasn't in the mood to argue anymore. She just wanted it to be over. She pulled out the files Steven had given her and began reading.

After Eddie left, Jamie returned to her room and got out her suitcase. She opened her dresser drawer and began pulling out shorts and t-shirts. When she reached the meerkat shirt Ben had given her at the zoo, she hugged it to her chest. She longed for that sense of happiness and freedom again. Jamie added it to her suitcase.

She cleaned out her refrigerator, took out the trash, and stopped in to tell the neighbors she and Eddie would be gone so they would keep an eye on the house. She didn't mention they wouldn't be going together.

While preparing for bed, Jamie removed her wedding ring and placed it in the wall safe. She felt as if she were closing the door on a part of her life. She wouldn't cry anymore for Eddie and her marriage. She would focus on the challenges ahead.

The next morning, Jamie drove by the post office and had her mail forwarded to the hotel in Virginia. She didn't know how long she'd be gone but only planned on coming home a few weekends to do things around the house.

As she drove the four hours south, she had a lot to think about. She wasn't sorry things were over with Eddie. She had been unhappy for some time now and was tired of trying so hard all the time.

Her thoughts kept drifting to Ben. Was a relationship with him now an option? She had made a fool of herself when he rejected her. Actually, thinking back on his words, he had said, "Not tonight." Did that mean there was a chance on another night? Jamie hung on to the hope of a second chance and smiled.

By the time she pulled into the Westin, her attitude was improving. She unpacked her clothes, slipped into shorts and a t-shirt, and headed for the gym. She was going to get her new life started on the right track.

"What do you mean she's gone?" Ben asked Carolyn.

"Mr. Hardy sent her to the Virginia Beach office."

"For how long?" Ben couldn't believe it. Jamie had left and hadn't said anything to him.

"He wasn't sure. They're having problems down there, and he felt Jamie could fix them. She'll be back. She isn't being replaced or anything," Carolyn said.

Ben left the office feeling depressed. They hadn't exactly parted on the best of terms, and now he didn't know when he was going to see her again. He thought about calling her but didn't know what he'd say. Perhaps he should wait until she called him.

Jamie threw herself into her work. Steven was right when he said they had problems here. He had only been shown the top layer. The more Jamie dug, the more dirt she found. It was all circling back to one or two people.

After a few weeks, she had her suspicions, but something was bugging her. It was as if she were missing a piece of the puzzle. She still had many more interviews to conduct and documentation to create if she were to properly ferret out the troublemaker.

The posts on Facebook were some of the most troubling evidence. Jamie had been directed to the Facebook account of Scott Jansen by more than one of the workers in his department.

The account had numerous pictures of Scott in various poses with women, some from his office, some not. Some were pictures of the women alone. No words with the pictures but they were numbered and scored. He was keeping his little black book electronically and sharing it freely. He had it open to the public. When Jamie last checked, it had twenty-six women's pictures with scores one through ten. There were no names and no criteria attached to the scoring system. Just the single digit (there were no tens) in bold font.

Trina slid into the booth across from Ben at the local sandwich shop that was a favorite of many of the Winkler and Stein crowd. "How's it going?"

Ben offered her a weak smile. "Never better," he said, taking a bite of his sandwich.

She overlooked his apathy and waved to get the waitress' attention. "Well, I'm going to make it better for you," she said.

Ben waited patiently for the explanation as Trina ordered her lunch. When she finished, she flashed him a dazzling smile. "We're going to a football game."

She paused, waiting for his reaction. When she didn't get what she hoped for, she hurriedly explained. "Sunday. It's the Washington Redskins versus the Cowboys. We have tickets on the fifty-yard line."

Now she had Ben's attention. His face lit up. "We do? Really? How did you score such great tickets?"

Trina rested her hand on his. "A girl doesn't reveal her sources."

"Well, however you got them, thanks for including me. Who else is going?"

Her smile faltered. "Just us. I thought it would be a nice change of pace."

Ben wasn't sure what she meant, but they were fifty-yard line tickets. He wasn't going to complain.

"Super. What time do you want me to pick you up?" Ben asked.

For the rest of their lunch, Trina and Ben made plans for the game on Sunday and a party Trina wanted to stop in at afterwards.

Jamie knocked on the office door.

A nice-looking man in his late twenties dressed in a charcoal suit looked up from behind an oak desk.

"Mr. Jansen?"

Standing, Scott walked around his desk and offered his hand which Jamie accepted. "Ms. Woods, I've been expecting you." He gestured toward one of the two chairs in front of his desk, and he took the other one.

Openness—not putting the desk as a barrier between us. This is good, Jamie thought.

"Thanks for seeing me, Mr. Jansen."

"Scott. Please. I'm actually glad you're here." He ran a hand through his short cropped, dark hair and sighed. "I want someone to get to the bottom of this and clear my name."

"Clear your name from what?" Jamie asked, trying to get his side of the story.

"My friends are distancing themselves from me. The women in this building are suspicious of my every move, and even my boss is starting to doubt my recommendations."

"Well you have to admit, you've made some pretty poor choices."

"That's what I mean! *I* haven't made the poor choices. Someone is setting me up."

"Setting you up?" Jamie asked.

Scott shook his head. "I didn't post anything on Facebook. I don't have an account. I don't even *read* Facebook."

Jamie was skeptical.

"I've emailed Facebook. I told them I want the page taken down. They said if I don't have the password, I can't make changes. They said even with a password, I could change things but not delete them; only hide them. It's insane." Scott was frustrated.

"The profile fits your history—your high school, college, fraternity. And you are in quite a few of the pictures."

"That doesn't prove anything. Anyone could have set up the account. Facebook doesn't care."

Jamie had to admit she wasn't a Facebook expert by any means. As a Human Resource Specialist, she searched Facebook when people applied for positions within Winkler and Stein to establish if they had posted anything to contradict what they put on their resume, but she never posted anything about herself. Most posts she read were benign to downright boring. She couldn't figure out the excitement behind it all.

"Why would someone want to set up an account with your information?"

Scott folded his hands together and leaned forward. "I don't know. To cause me grief, I guess. And it's working."

"Are you telling me you haven't dated the women on your site?"

"It's not *my* site!" He sat back and shook his head again. "Yes, I have been out with a few of those women, but not all of them. And none since the postings started. Now I'm a social pariah."

After another hour of discussion, Jamie left Scott in his office and went back to her borrowed cubicle. She opened up her laptop and typed www.facebook.com into the address line on Internet Explorer.

Within minutes she had created an account for Jane Doe living in San Diego, California. She was amazed there were no checks or balances in place. She understood how this could be dangerous.

But she had to be careful. She would be fair to Scott and concede someone else could have set up the account. But it could also be just as true he set up the account and was now blaming it on someone else. After all, it did have pictures of him with women he had dated.

Jamie refilled her cup at the office coffee bar. She was lost in her thoughts. Trying to balance the work from her D.C. office while untangling this mystery was harder than she thought. Luckily, Carolyn had been doing a great job passing off the more routine work to others in Jamie's division and only forwarding the finished projects for final review. Still, it made for very long days.

As she added creamer to her coffee, she heard someone enter. She turned and offered a smile to the newcomer. "Good morning."

"Good morning. You're a new face. Are you Jamie Woods, by any chance?"

"I am. And you are?" She extended her hand.

"Susan Collins," she said, taking Jamie's hand. Susan was dressed in a dark business suit, open-collared blouse, and a twisted gold chain around her neck. She was on the shorter side with a nice smile and open manner about her that Jamie warmed to right away.

"I work in sales. I heard you were here trying to straighten out the Jansen mess. We appreciate it."

"Who do you mean by 'we'?"

"A lot of the women here are getting a bad name because of the trash being talked. No one wants their personal life rated and posted for all to see. It's nice to know management isn't going to allow it to continue." Susan pulled a cup from the cupboard and poured herself some coffee.

Jamie motioned toward a table. "Want to sit for a while? I'd like to ask you a few more questions."

Susan confirmed the stories Jamie had been hearing from other women, and even some of the men, she had talked to. Scott Jansen was a bit of a ladies' man but not particularly obnoxious about it. He was also known as a jokester, and more than one person suggested the Facebook thing was something they wouldn't put past him. No one thought he was malicious or meant any harm but felt he had made an error in judgment and was afraid to come clean.

The women in the pictures from his site were embarrassed. Jamie got the impression they were more embarrassed they got low scores than they were for being on the list. A few complained Scott had no business rating them since they had done nothing more than go out for coffee.

Susan wasn't part of the little black book, but she knew some of the women who were. She said she had warned them not to date anyone from the office. "From my experience, office romances are doomed for failure," Susan commented.

Suddenly she changed the topic. "You work in the D.C. office, right? You must know Ben Simons."

Jamie was thrown off guard. She didn't expect to hear Ben's name so far from home. "Sure, I know Ben. How do you know him?"

Susan smiled impishly. "We dated for a while. I used to live in D.C. He helped me get this job, as a matter of fact." She got up to pour herself another cup of coffee. "How is he?" she asked without turning around.

This is the *Susan?* Jamie thought. She swallowed before answering. "He's fine. He's doing well."

"Is he dating anyone?" Susan was trying to be nonchalant, but she didn't fool Jamie.

"Not that I know of." Jamie was getting uncomfortable. "Were you serious?" She thought she knew the answer if this was the same Susan.

"I was. He wasn't. I don't know if Ben can get serious." There was a silence as both women contemplated the statement. "He's a great guy though. He could always make me laugh." Susan smiled. "I'd be rich if I had taken every quarter he offered me for my thoughts."

A knife twisted in Jamie's heart. For some reason, she thought the quarter idea was special between her and Ben. Silly thinking. Of course she wasn't special to him. He was single and had other women. He might even have a girlfriend now for all Jamie knew.

Jamie stood and excused herself to get back to work. She thanked Susan for the talk.

"Tell Ben I said hi."

"I will," Jamie assured her.

Chapter 21

When Ben picked Trina up for the game, he was surprised she was dressed in a Redskins maroon and gold sweater, tight jeans, and high heeled boots. "Think those heels are a good idea at the stadium?" Ben asked.

Trina glanced at her shoes and made a pouty face at Ben. "You don't like them?"

"They're fine," Ben answered. "I just think your feet are going to hurt before long."

"No, I love these boots."

"Where's your coat?"

"If I wear one, no one can see my sweater. I got it just for today."

Ben shrugged and opened the door, "Let's go then."

Trina talked the whole way to FedEx Field. Ben concentrated on the traffic and injected a statement once in a while.

He followed the stream of traffic exiting I-495 to Arena Drive. It was bumper to bumper but at least they continued to move. As they pulled onto FedEx Way, Trina clapped her hands with excitement.

"Look at the gorgeous building!" she exclaimed.

Ben wouldn't have used the term gorgeous, but it was quite a sight. The streetlights glittered off the glass panels lining the oblong structure. Above the eight rows of windows, the stadium seats reached toward the sky. He pitied the poor saps who had the nosebleed seats. He'd been there before, and the view wasn't worth the admission price. He thought about their tickets midfield and anxiously searched for a parking space.

By the time they reached the stadium, Ben was ready for a beer. He waited in line and took in the atmosphere. He hadn't been to a game in years. The smell of stale beer, hot dogs, and too many people filled his nostrils.

He watched an older man shuffle through the crowd with a broom and extra deep dustpan. The man would stop long enough to sweep up spilled popcorn or a flutter of napkins that got away from someone, and then he was on his way. Abstractly, Ben wondered if the man had to stay out here during the game or if he got to slip inside to watch.

"Next," he heard and turned to place his order.

He retrieved their beers and met Trina at their seats.

"This is great, Trina. Thanks again."

Trina took his arm. "No, thank you. I'm glad you could come."

As the game progressed, Ben noticed Trina was getting unsteady on her feet. He was unsure if it was the boots or the beer, but he suggested she sit and rest a while. "Only if you sit with me," she cooed.

Ben wasn't interested in sitting while the crowd stood around them, but he didn't want to be ungrateful. He sat and Trina leaned in close. "It is a little chilly, don't you think?" Trina asked.

"You can have my jacket," Ben offered, unzipping it.

"No, just share your body heat with me," Trina said, slipping her arms around him.

A cheer arose from the crowd, and Ben jumped up to see what he had missed. The Redskins had intercepted a pass, and Ben had to watch it on the instant replay screen.

He didn't know what Trina was playing, but he wasn't interested.

When the game was over, Ben held Trina's hand to lead her through the crowd. Her sore feet were slowing her down, but Ben wasn't showing mercy.

They got to the car, and Ben opened her door for her. She slipped into the seat and rubbed her arms to warm herself up.

Ben opened his door and slid behind the wheel. He started the car and waited while the heat kicked in. "That was a great game," he said.

Trina smiled brightly. "It was, wasn't it?" She tried not to shiver. "Let's stop by the party for a while and see who's there."

He steered through the throngs of people leaving the stadium and headed toward the highway. As Trina warmed up, so did her conversation. She turned partway in her seat and rested her hand on the back on Ben's seat. He glanced at her, and she smiled innocently back.

"You aren't talking much tonight. Why don't you tell me more about yourself outside of work?" she said.

Ben shifted uncomfortably and kept his eyes on the road. "What's there to tell? I grew up in Pennsylvania, went to school in New York, worked in New York for a while and have been with Winkler and Stein for five years."

"Any pets?"

He grinned. "No pets, no plants, no ties. That's always worked well for me."

Trina was quiet, probably thinking about her next question, when they pulled up in front of the house. One of the guys in Trina's department was throwing a victory party for the Redskins. He had placed a big bet they would win. Luckily, he was right.

When they walked in the door, the host greeted Trina with a peck on the cheek and offered them both a drink.

Ben and Trina followed him to the bar where he mixed up his specialty. Ben was afraid to ask what was in it, but it tasted pretty good.

Trina kicked off her boots and headed for the makeshift dance floor. The music was loud, and Ben was happy to sit back and people watch. There were a number of people from work at the party but more who Ben didn't recognize. There were even a few women from the Liberty Tavern.

One particularly striking redhead approached him with an extra drink in hand. "You're a gin and tonic man, right?" she asked as she handed it to him.

Surprised, he accepted and made room for her next to him on the couch. "How did you know?"

"You've ordered from me plenty of times." She had a beautiful smile that had seen its share of dental work. "I work at Liberty."

"Sorry, I didn't recognize you in this setting."

"Don't worry about it. Where's the woman you're always hanging around with?" she asked, glancing around.

Ben hid his embarrassment with a drink. He never put much thought into the fact that others might notice how much time Jamie and he spent together.

"Not sure who you mean," Ben said.

"The woman with reddish-brown hair. I haven't seen her lately."

"You must mean Jamie. She's in Virginia Beach on business."

"So you're alone?"

"Sort of," he said glancing around for Trina. She was dancing with a group of people but looking in his direction.

The redhead smiled and raised her drink. "Here's to a different setting," she said.

Chapter 22

As Ben drove Trina home, he sensed something was bothering her. "What's up? You're awfully quiet."

Trina leaned over the console and took his arm.

Uh oh, thought Ben.

Her fingers ran delicately up and down his arm.

He knew she consumed over her limit of alcohol so he had to tread carefully to avoid a situation they would both regret later.

"I saw you with that redhead," Trina said.

Ben stayed silent.

"Do you prefer redheads?"

"I have no preferences," Ben answered, although Jamie's face flashed into his mind.

"Then why are you so hard to get close to?" Trina's hand moved to his thigh. "Are you afraid of getting close?" Her words slurred.

"I'm just not interested in a relationship right now." Ben tried to let her down gently. He liked Trina. She was fun to be around and a good friend of Jamie's.

"So maybe you only like the ones who can't tie you down."

He didn't answer.

"Safe ones," she continued as she stroked his leg, "like Jamie."

For a moment, Ben's breathing stopped and the muscles on his leg tightened. Trina must have noticed because she looked intently at his profile.

"So that's it. You and Jamie have something going on." She removed her hand and sat back in the seat. "You'd think she would have at least told me."

"There's nothing going on with us," Ben assured her.

"That's not what your body language says." She was lost in thought for a moment. "It explains a lot, actually."

Ben wasn't sure how to react. He didn't want to reignite her interest in him, but he also didn't want to start rumors at the office about him and Jamie.

"Jamie and I are just friends. You're right. Maybe she's safe because we both know we'll never be more than friends. That's all I can handle right now."

Trina kept her thoughts to herself as she watched the houses float passed out the window.

"Howdy, stranger."

There was a slight delay and then Jamie heard, "Well, hello, yourself."

God, it's good to hear his voice, she thought. A sudden shyness overtook her, and she wasn't sure what to say next.

"You still there?" Ben asked.

"I'm here."

"I thought we got disconnected for a minute. It's good to hear from you."

There was so much Jamie wanted to tell him but didn't know where to start.

"How's the investigation going? Steve told me he has you on a special project... since *no one* else decided to fill me in." Ben couldn't resist the jab.

"Yeah, sorry about that. It all happened so fast. I was trying to finish things up at the office and pack for an unspecified amount of time. It just slipped my mind," she said sheepishly.

He let her off the hook. "So? Have you solved the mystery?"

"Not really. It doesn't add up."

"What do you mean?"

"It's too obvious. It doesn't make sense that this guy would tell stories outside the bedroom about sleeping with a co-worker, knowing it would spread like wildfire. Especially *multiple* co-workers."

"Maybe the simple answer is the answer."

Now it was Jamie's turn to be confused. "Okay, I'll bite. What are you getting at?"

"Maybe he didn't say them."

"But the women certainly didn't tell anyone. They claim none of it's true. Who else would say something so hateful?"

"Who else benefits?"

"He wasn't in a position to affect any of the women's standing in the company. There were no job openings or promotions pending. He wasn't high enough in the food chain for anyone to be vying for his job."

"You're thinking too much like a professional. Think on the personal level," Ben prodded.

A light bulb went on in Jamie's head. "Ben, you're a genius."

"I've been telling you that since I've known you," he said.

"But this time *I'm* saying it." Jamie was excited. And she knew just the person she was going to talk to in the morning.

That reminded her. "I ran into a friend of yours down here," Jamie ventured.

"Oh? Who?"

"Susan Collins."

Jamie could hear the smile in his voice. "Tell her I said hi. How's she doing these days? Does she like Virginia Beach?"

Jamie wasn't sure what she expected, but this wasn't it. She thought he would be taken off guard or embarrassed or something. His total ease of discussing an old girlfriend with her told Jamie he was treating her like one of the guys.

Of course he wouldn't be surprised Susan was here. He helped her get the job. He knew where she was. *Probably already knew how she liked the beach too*, Jamie thought snidely.

"She's doing great. She wanted me to tell you hi too." Trying to match his casual tone, she said, "She also wanted to know if you were dating anyone."

The seconds dragged before Ben answered, "What did you tell her?"

"No one important," Jamie answered.

"Well, that's not exactly true," Ben said before he could censor himself. "I mean, not officially."

Jamie had heard enough. "Well, thanks for your help on this. You shed light on some things." And she wasn't just talking about her issues at work.

"I'm here for you anytime. Don't wait so long to call next time."

"Good night," she said, hanging up before he could say anything else.

The following week at work, Jamie tracked Susan down. "Susan, you know a lot of what goes on around here," Jamie began.

Susan smiled and waved her hand in the air. "When you don't have a social life, you tend to thrive on hearing about others."

"Is there anyone who's paid special interest to Scott?"

"To Scott? In what way? I mean, everyone is talking about his Facebook page."

"I'm thinking maybe I've been coming at this from the wrong angle. What if the purpose of the trash talk wasn't to hurt the women? What if it's to hurt Scott?"

Susan thought about it.

Jamie went on, "Is there someone he might have gone out with only once or twice and then not again? Or someone who wanted to go out with him who he didn't pay any attention to?"

"Off the top of my head, I can only think of one woman who isn't a big fan of Scott. Besides the general irritation at his stupidity over the Facebook, that is."

"Who?"

"Cathy McMullin. She's a piece of work herself."

"Why do you say that?" Jamie asked.

"After word got out about the Facebook posts, I admit, I checked them out. I was curious about who was on there. Cathy wasn't one of them, but she was always talking about the site to anyone who would listen. A real bore. It was as if she were a Facebook lurker."

That was a new term to Jamie, and it must have shown in her expression.

"Someone who doesn't post, but just pokes around reading other people's posts. It's common," Susan said.

Guess I fit into the lurker category, Jamie thought. For work, she often read posts but had no intention of putting news of her life out in the open.

"One day at lunch, Cathy was going on about the Facebook posts and slamming Scott for being such a pig toward women," Susan said. She tilted her head to the left and stared off into space in deep concentration. "I'll bet Scott is the *he* she was pissed at," she said under her breath.

Jamie was confused.

Susan made a back-up motion with her hands and started again. "I was out with some friends from the office one night when Cathy started mouthing off. She had been pounding drinks pretty hard and was overly emotional. We tried to calm her down, but she wouldn't stop. She started ranting about how *he* didn't know what he was missing."

Jamie got excited. This might be the piece she had been lacking.

"We pretty much ignored her. She was recently divorced and had a tendency to hit on guys regularly, so we didn't think much about it. She wouldn't tell us who 'he' was anyway."

Jamie sipped her coffee, dying to ask questions, but not wanting to interrupt the story.

"Then she got it stuck in her head there must be another woman involved. Cathy couldn't admit a guy wasn't interested in her. She was convinced no one would turn her down if she turned on her charm. She even claimed she could get a straight woman to turn gay if she wanted to."

They laughed together as Susan got up to refill her coffee.

"Do you think Cathy had her sights on Scott?" Jamie asked.

Susan shrugged. "She's way too hostile toward him to not care at all."

Jamie understood that concept well. In her college psychology classes, the professors often talked about the fine line between love and hate. They are both such strong emotions. A person wouldn't typically waste time hating someone they didn't care about deeply.

She thanked Susan for her insight and headed back to her hotel early. She had a lot to assimilate and needed uninterrupted time to think.

By the time she had finished her run, a plan had begun to form in her mind.

Chapter 23

After a few days of confirming her theory, Jamie called to update Steven. "I knew women could be catty, but I've never seen anything this bad."

"What do you mean?"

"I suspect there's one particular person behind this, but I'm not going to name names until I tie up a few loose ends."

"Are you going to at least give me a hint as to what's going on?" he pressed.

Jamie painted the picture for Steven. "It comes down to unrequited attraction. There's a particular female—a junior executive, I'm sorry to say—who had the hots for one of her coworkers. He wasn't interested and let her down easily from all accounts, but for some reason she couldn't accept it gracefully.

"Remember the fox and the sour grapes? Well, instead of just pretending she didn't want him, she tried to make it so no one else would want him either. In her mud flinging, a number of innocent people got smeared along the way."

"Hmmmm, sounds like one of your skits," Steven observed.

"Good idea," Jamie laughed. Then she turned serious again. "But it gets worse. The unwanted woman started rumors that the object of her affections turned her down because he was sleeping with another person in the company. Of course it wasn't true, so when this report didn't grow legs, she decided to fan the flames with more outrageous claims. Now he's credited with sleeping with multiple women at the same time…and boasting about it on Facebook!"

Jamie heard a sigh on the other end of the phone and could picture Steven shaking his head in disbelief. She didn't imagine he had a Facebook page but was pretty sure his teenage daughters did, so he was no stranger to the social media frenzy.

She continued, "By this time there were enough people whispering about it that some started to consider it. The rumors spread. I talked to a lot of people. Most claim they didn't believe the tales themselves, but they enjoyed speculating, so the stories continued.

"As you can imagine, the man's reputation wasn't suffering for sleeping around—until the posts on Facebook started. After that, no woman wanted to be his next target, so they started avoiding him. And not just women from the office."

"Why didn't the offended women come forward sooner?" Steven asked.

"They complained to their superiors, but they were helpless to combat whispers. And there weren't any words on the Facebook posts to argue over…just numbers. There was a lot of bickering and finger pointing."

"It's a shame it got so out of hand. We'll have to think of a way to nip this in the bud, in case there's a next time." Steven was silent as he thought it through. "Well, one step at a time, I guess. Where do you go from here?"

"I'm afraid to have to break this to you, but I think someone is going to lose her job over this. I want to make sure I document everything carefully. I need some hard proof."

"I understand. Take all the time you need. I knew you were the right person to tackle this."

"Besides, you figured selecting a female to handle the situation would help dispel rumors of unfair treatment." Jamie could see through the bullshit and would call it as she saw it—no matter who was involved.

Eve Jordan. Twenty-eight, blonde hair, green eyes, Cherokee High School in Santa Fe, New Mexico. Jamie typed rapidly. She was still amazed it was so easy to create a new identity from nothing.

She went out to a website where she could get free stock photos and downloaded a picture of a female fitting the description she had designed. She posted a few bogus posts beside her fake photo. Over the next few days, she built up a small history.

She even went so far as to create a few other characters and carried on fake conversations with herself, just to make Eve appear more real. She had to laugh when she received a few friend requests from real people who went to "her" high school and wanted to reconnect. One person tried to convince her they sat next to each other in geometry class.

A few days later, and many more posts, it was time to put her plan into action. "Eve" sent a private message to Scott using his false Facebook account. "I can't wait to see you tonight! I'll wear something special, just for you! I can be your 10!"

Then on Eve's Facebook wall, she posted a note for her "friends." She signed off and went back to her paperwork. She hoped this would work because she was ready to go home.

Cathy's email pinged. She was surprised to see Scott's Facebook account had received an email. She had set up the account using a phony Gmail account but had anything going there forwarded to her at work so she could monitor it.

At first, some of the women she had posted about wrote back nasty messages and denials about any sexual encounters. They tapered off because "Scott" never responded. It had been a while since she had received any emails.

"I can't wait to see you tonight! I'll wear something special, just for you! I can be your 10!" she read. Jealousy flashed. *He really was seeing someone else!*

"That bastard!" she hissed. She started to hit reply to cancel the date but caught herself. She was on her work computer, not the forged Facebook account.

She took a deep breath and deleted the email. She glanced around the office to see if anyone was nearby. It was lunchtime so the cubicles were mostly empty. She opened Facebook and typed in her password. Scott's smiling face appeared, and she searched who had recently friended Scott. She clicked on the link to Eve Jordan and "Scott" accepted her as a friend.

Cathy had never seen her before. *It figures he would go for a blonde,* she thought as she inspected the photos. Eve's top post caught her eye.

"Tonight is going to be special. I'm seeing Scott again. Wish me luck! In the morning, I'll let you know how it goes. He says he has something to ask me!" It was followed by goofy smiley face symbols and other emoticons demonstrating excitement.

Cathy silenced the scream that wanted to escape her throat. How could any woman be stupid enough to want a man as perverted as she had portrayed Scott to be?

As Jamie untangled the mess at work, her personal life was unraveling. By the beginning of her third month gone, she received the promised papers from the lawyer and read them over. They had no children, so the courts weren't going to get involved too much. The settlement was straight down the middle; Jamie couldn't complain. She signed the papers and put the pen down with finality. She couldn't believe it was over. She never thought she would be a statistic.

She decided to treat herself to an extra nice dinner to celebrate a new beginning. She didn't feel much like celebrating but thought if she went through the motions, it would come to pass.

The night air was cool as Jamie walked to a restaurant recommended by the hotel concierge. She cinched her jacket around her waist tightly and increased her pace.

As she entered the restaurant, warm air greeted her. Jamie heard the sound of a piano being played nearby but couldn't immediately locate the source. Her eyes roamed over the spacious entryway and past the hostess to see a baby grand piano in the center of the dining room. The open black lid blocked her view of the very talented pianist at the keys.

The hostess led her to a table near the window. Jamie sat staring at the couples walking by arm in arm. She sighed and turned away, focusing on the menu.

The waiter brought bread and water to the table. Jamie ordered a gin and tonic. As he walked away, she cursed her choice. Why did she have the taste for gin and tonic? It wasn't her usual drink; but it was Ben's, when he wasn't in the mood for a beer.

Jamie examined the menu but found she wasn't hungry. She decided on a salad and set the menu aside. The piano player must have taken a break because she now heard piped music coming from speakers hidden in the ceiling. It was too loud for background music. The flutes and strings were meant to give a relaxed feel, but at this volume, they seemed to be hurrying people along.

Jamie watched the shoppers out the window and wondered what she should do for Christmas. Maybe she'd spend it with her mother. She could count on her mom to spoil her in an attempt to raise her spirits after her divorce. She hadn't gone into the details with her mother about how things fell apart, but she hadn't needed to either. Betty had confided she recognized things weren't quite right for some time now but knew Jamie had to figure it out for herself. Well, Jamie was still trying to sort it all out.

As she finished her salad, the waitress brought over a cocktail, relaying it had been purchased for her by a young man. Jamie's heart raced as she searched for Ben in the restaurant. A nice-looking gentleman in a gray sports jacket raised his drink to her. She smiled appreciatively and waved, trying to hide her disappointment.

The man took that as approval for him to approach. Jamie didn't know how to get out of it. She was so out of practice at this scene. He held out his hand and introduced himself, "I'm Sal Quint. Nice to meet you."

"I'm Jamie," she said, not willing to give up her last name.

"May I join you?" he asked.

Jamie consented, although she wasn't in the mood for small talk.

"I hope you don't mind," Sal said. "I'm not generally this forward, but you look lonely." He hesitated then went on. "Okay, truth is, I'm lonely and I hoped you'd take pity on me. My flight out of Norfolk got delayed a few hours, and so I'm stuck eating dinner alone instead of with sixty strangers on a crowded airplane. Food is always better when shared, don't you think?"

Jamie forced a smile. "Desserts are better when you don't have to share."

"But if two people get different desserts, then you get both tastes with the calories of only one dessert."

Jamie had to laugh at his reasoning. "Okay, you got me. But you have to get something with chocolate."

She was glad she had invited him to stay for dinner after all. Sal was good company and pushed aside the melancholy feeling that hovered around her so often over the last few years.

Ben would like this guy, Jamie caught herself thinking. *Damn*, was her next thought. Her life didn't revolve around Ben, but he was always on her mind. She felt guilty for slighting Sal. He was charming in his own way, but Jamie continually found herself comparing him to Ben. This couldn't be healthy.

Before they had a chance to order dessert, Jamie signaled the waiter for the check. "I'm sorry. I have to work tomorrow and I'm exhausted. It was very nice of you to keep me company though."

Disappointment showed on his face. "It was my pleasure. And my treat," he scooped up the black padded bi-fold as the waiter set it on the table.

"You don't have to do that," Jamie protested.

"It's the least I can do. I barged in on your evening." Sal slid his gold American Express into the folder and handed it back to the waiter standing nearby.

While they waited, Sal said, "You don't owe me anything for dinner, but I would love to call you next time I'm in town."

She squirmed. It was times like this she would love to be able to flash her wedding ring and be done with guys hitting on her. She went with the honest approach. "I'm newly divorced and not real interested in dating just yet."

"Well, your ex really screwed up to let you go," he said looking her in the eyes. "Don't let him ruin your future too by making you think all guys are that stupid." He smiled at her and relaxed back in his chair. "You'll find someone who will appreciate you. Give yourself time."

She smiled in gratitude and reached across the table to squeeze his hand. "Thanks for restoring my faith in mankind," she kidded as she stood. "It was nice to meet you. Have a good flight."

Chapter 24

The next morning, Jamie went to work with a sense of anticipation. Hopefully today she would be able to tie things up. She arrived early and checked in with the IT department.

Although Jamie wasn't an expert at information technology, she knew what they were capable of. She remembered signing the agreement when she joined the firm allowing the company to monitor her use of the computer. Most people never thought twice about it. The management wasn't looking for people who checked their personal email over lunch. They were more concerned with ensuring the employees weren't going on porn sites or playing war games.

Jamie was going to use this consent to her advantage.

"Good morning," she said cheerily as she entered the cool room in the basement of the building. She put a box of doughnuts on the table and pulled out a chair.

"Good morning. Did you bring anything healthy?" the technician asked, glancing at the box.

"No way. This is like a stakeout. Cops don't eat healthy on a stakeout."

He laughed. "You know, I don't think what she has done is illegal." He stood and stretched. The paunch belly hanging over his belt told Jamie she had made the right choice with the doughnuts.

"Fred, I don't have to have her arrested. I just need to ensure I'm right about my hunch. The standards of proof are a lot lower than needed in a court of law."

Fred pointed at a computer monitor. "That is set up to ghost her system. You'll see what she sees."

"Are you capturing her keystrokes?"

"Yes, ma'am. We can print them out whenever you want them." He reached into the box. "Did you at least bring fruit-filled? Fruit's good for you."

Jamie shook her head with a smile and turned to the monitor. She leaned back and put her feet up on a nearby chair. It might be a long day of waiting if she was wrong.

Jamie checked her watch again. It was eight o'clock. Cathy should be at work by now. She didn't want to post the results of her date with Scott too early. She wanted to make sure Cathy used her work computer to check the status.

There. Jamie could see through the ghost computer Cathy had logged in. She tossed her magazine aside and pulled the keyboard closer. She opened Eve's Facebook page and began her post.

"*What a night!! He'll post a 10 for me for sure.* <smile>"

Jamie opened another window on the browser and logged into Facebook as one of her other characters. From there, she went to Eve's wall and posted, *"TELL ME! What did he ask you?"*

Jamie was feeling a little schizophrenic as she flipped between her characters. She wanted to make Eve come alive, so she kept the dialogue banter going back and forth for a few posts.

A flicker on Cathy's ghost computer caught her eye. She was opening a browser. She was going to Facebook!

"Are you getting this?" Jamie asked the technician.

"I got it."

Jamie was excited as she watched Scott's Facebook page open. It was eerie watching the computer cursor move on its own across the screen. "Scott" clicked on Eve's page. Jamie watched as Eve's picture was copied from her page and the screen jumped back to Scott's page. The picture was posted in a new message, and the writing appeared on the screen. *"#27."*

Jamie recognized the next number in the counting sequence of Scott's supposed conquests.

"*2*," she read next, as "Scott" rated Eve's performance from the night before.

Jamie laughed out loud. Fred looked over at her. She waved him off.

Jamie approached the cubicle where Cathy was intently studying the monitor. She read over her shoulder as Cathy clicked through pages of Facebook, trying to trace some of Eve's friends.

"You know you aren't supposed to be using work computers for personal web surfing," Jamie said, causing Cathy to jump.

She stabbed at the power button on the monitor and stood to face Jamie. "I was on break. The boss doesn't mind."

Jamie pulled up a seat beside her uninvited and set a folder on the desk. "You know what the boss *does* mind?" she asked in a friendly tone. She didn't wait for a reply. "People stirring up trouble."

Cathy took her seat again and looked at her without answering.

"Have you heard about Scott's Facebook page? It's caused a lot of trouble." This time Jamie waited out the silence that grew between them but kept an approachable expression on her face.

Cathy gave in with a shrug. "He's a bit of a snake for writing about those poor women. Why doesn't the boss do something about it?" She tried to relax, but Jamie could see the sweat forming on her forehead.

"He is doing something. He sent me here." Again, silence.

"And? How's it going?" Cathy was trying to act indifferent but wasn't quite pulling it off.

"It's going great, actually." Jamie sat back in her chair and crossed her legs. "I finally figured out why he set up the website."

Jamie caught Cathy's barely perceptible sigh of relief. "So why did he?"

"Inferiority. It was a pathetic attempt to regain some control he never had to begin with."

"What do you mean?" Cathy asked.

"Have you ever heard of unrequited love? You know, liking someone so much, but they weren't interested in you? It makes you feel powerless. I've felt that way before. It's the sense I got when I looked at Scott's Facebook page. Whoever would come up with that crap was dying for attention."

Cathy shifted in her seat uncomfortably but stopped herself from speaking.

"I did a lot of asking around about Scott. Everyone likes him. He has many friends and had a fairly successful romantic life until recently." She brushed an imaginary crumb from her slacks and looked around the room. "It occurred to me he had no reason to feel powerless. His life was looking pretty good."

Cathy couldn't help herself. "Obviously his romantic life was good. Look at all the women he posted about."

Jamie leaned forward again, "But that's just it. The kind of person who would post trash like a numbering scale is an insecure, jealous type. Not confident and happy like Scott. He isn't even arrogant." She let it sink in. "No, I think it was someone else using Scott's name."

Cathy swallowed hard. "Who would do something like that?"

"I was hoping you could help me figure it out. I hear you asked Scott out, and he turned you down."

"That's a lie!" she spat out before she could stop herself.

"Oh? Maybe you want to give me your side of the story."

Cathy stood. "This is crazy. I don't have to talk to you about my personal life."

Jamie remained sitting and calmly said, "Sit down, Cathy." She looked up with icy eyes and held her gaze.

Cathy sank back into her chair under the draw of Jamie's stare.

Now Jamie's pleasant expression was gone, replaced by one of determination. "I hear you made quite a scene after Scott turned you down. Ranting and raving with co-workers. You see, *that's* a sign of insecurity."

Cathy was shaking; whether out of fear or anger, Jamie wasn't sure. She went on, "I think you need to learn how to accept when things don't go your way."

"I haven't done anything wrong," Cathy stammered.

"Wrong is a subjective term. But I don't think you could convince anyone there was anything *right* about setting up a phony Facebook page in Scott's name to punish him for not wanting to go out with you." Jamie couldn't resist. She had to add, "Seems to me like he made the right choice."

Cathy was outraged. "I didn't set up his Facebook page."

"Well, technology says otherwise." Jamie reached for the folder she had placed on the desk and opened it to reveal a stack of papers. "It's amazing the tools the IT department has at their disposal these days." She handed Cathy the papers.

Cathy's face turned white as she recognized familiar words amidst the garble of other signs and symbols on the page—words she had typed on her computer just that morning. "Where did you get this? You have no right—"

Jamie cut her off. She produced another sheet of paper with Cathy's signature on the bottom. "Actually, I do have the right. You gave it to me when you signed this consent to monitoring when you accepted your job. You need to learn to read before you sign."

"How dare you!" Cathy's voice was elevating, and a crowd of onlookers were starting to gather. "I'm going to sue you and Winkler and Stein!" Her words were strong, but her pitch was starting to waver.

"You could waste your money trying." Jamie kept her voice low but firm. She didn't want to make a scene. "But your best bet is to gather your personal belongings and walk out the door with a little dignity. Winkler and Stein no longer requires your services."

Cathy stared in disbelief. "What are you saying? I can't lose my job over this. Not over a guy! And certainly not over Scott!"

As she sat in shock, Jamie continued, "I need your building pass."

Cathy glanced at the faces surrounding her. "What are you staring at?" she snapped. The people suddenly remembered they had other places to be and moved on.

Cathy reached under the desk for her purse and pulled out the laminated badge giving her access to the offices after hours and flung it at Jamie. "You can't fire me over a harmless prank. My lawyer is going to have a field day with this."

Jamie didn't bother to answer. She stood and motioned for Cathy to stand also. For the first time, Cathy noticed the security guard standing against the wall a few cubicles away. He was watching her.

"Afraid I was going to hurt you?" she asked with a condescending air, gesturing to the guard.

"I think things through better than you do. I don't take unnecessary chances."

Cathy grabbed her purse and threw a few personal items in it from her desktop. "This isn't over," she growled.

"I imagine it isn't," Jamie said in a bored tone.

Jamie followed Cathy as she stormed out of the office and down the hallway. She made sure Cathy was out of the building before turning to the security guard. "Make sure she is removed from the employee list, and everyone knows she can't be in the building unescorted."

The guard nodded and walked to the parking lot to watch Cathy's car speed out of the lot.

When she got back to her room, she thought about calling Ben. She was dying to tell him about her sting operation, and it was a great excuse to connect with him. She was still a little frail after their last talk and hearing him mention someone else in his life, but she was hoping the topic of her divorce would somehow come up, and she could get his reaction on it.

She rehearsed how she might casually drop it in the conversation. "Guess what I got in the mail the other day?"

She knew that was the wrong approach, but she wasn't sure what else she could do. She also wanted to apologize for not calling more often. But then again, he hadn't called her either. He'd probably been too busy.

Someone had to take the first step. The ping-pong ball in her head was maddening. She opened her small refrigerator and pulled out a bottle of white wine. She had been nursing it over the past week. Now she needed it to steel her nerves. As she sipped wine from the hotel water glass, she decided the first step was just to make the phone call. Maybe the topic of Eddie would come up on its own.

She gulped down the last bit if her wine and picked up the phone. She found his number in her contacts and pressed the dial button. The phone rang three times and went to voice mail.

Chapter 25

Ben walked into Liberty Tavern. He wasn't in the mood to socialize, but people would talk if he stopped going to First Fridays because Jamie wasn't there.

He was still hurt he hadn't heard from her. He didn't know how much longer she would be gone but took her silence as a bad sign. Obviously, he wasn't as important to her as he had hoped.

He went to the bar and ordered a gin and tonic. While he waited, a young blonde slipped up next to him to order a drink. She smiled at him politely and placed her order.

"Do you work around here?" she asked.

Ben turned to face her, one elbow resting on the bar. "Not far. You?"

"I just started at Saltgrass. It's been a tough week, and I definitely needed a drink."

Ben laughed. "I would think coming to the competition's bar would be the last place you'd want to be."

"Are you kidding? I want someone to wait on me for a change."

When the bartender returned with her drink, Ben added it to his tab.

"Thanks," she said, holding up her glass. They clinked. "Want to join me at a table?"

Ben hesitated.

"Come on. I won't bite. It's better than leaning on the bar."

He followed her to a table where they chatted easily. Sarah had an infectious laugh, and Ben had to admit he was enjoying himself.

As they talked, his eyes were drawn to the low cut of her blouse and the smooth skin it exposed. He tried to keep his eyes raised, but it was a distraction.

"Hey, Ben," Trina said, pulling up a chair. "Who's your new friend?"

Ben made the introductions. Trina gave Sarah the once over before shaking her hand. "The Saltgrass, eh? Never been there. Is it worth it?"

Sarah finished off her drink. "It's nice enough. Gets loud on Saturday nights with a live band."

"Big dance floor?"

"Yep. And packed."

"I'll have to check it out," Trina said, signaling the waitress to bring another round.

Trina turned to Ben. "Have you heard from Jamie?"

Ben's happy mood evaporated. "Nope." He took a long swig to finish his drink.

Trina waited for more, but Ben had clammed up.

"Who's Jamie?" Sarah asked.

When Ben didn't reply, Trina offered, "A friend of ours from work who's working a special project in Virginia Beach."

"Lucky her," Sarah said. "I love Virginia Beach, even in the winter."

Trina and Sarah exchanged stories about various vacations they had been on. Ben didn't join in the conversation, but he listened, smiling at humorous anecdotes.

By ten o'clock, and several drinks later, Ben's mood had improved. Trina had wandered off with some other friends, leaving Ben and Sarah alone.

Sarah reached across the table and touched Ben's hand. "How about getting out of here?" she asked.

Jamie's face flashed across his vision. He saw her eyes sparkling when she smiled and could hear her laughter. Then he saw the light in her eyes fade and the pain take over when she reinforced the fact that she was married.

They couldn't be together. He couldn't have her to himself, and although it was tempting to push the envelope, he didn't want to put her in an awkward position again. He needed to forget about any kind of romantic future with her. He wanted her to come home though.

Ben motioned for the check.

As they left the bar, Sarah slipped her hand into Ben's. Ben wavered, but in the end, gave in. He had nothing to lose.

Jamie lay back on the bed and kicked herself. It was First Friday. Why did she expect him to pick up the phone? Trina was probably there with him. Jamie was sure she hadn't lost any time making her moves. The few emails she received from Trina while she was gone were benign. Work stuff mostly, although she made sure to mention Ben had taken her to a football game and a party afterward.

Jamie didn't think Trina was his type, but she was attractive, and they all got along great. She didn't see anything permanent coming out of it, but after talking to Susan, perhaps Ben wasn't looking for permanent.

Ben woke up a little groggy from the night's drinking. As he tried to put together the pieces, he looked around at his unfamiliar surroundings. A slender arm rested across his bare chest. He took in the rest of Sarah's body covered in nothing but a sheet. He passed his hand over his face and rubbed his eyes. An incredible feeling of guilt washed over him.

The guilt was two-fold. He felt like he was cheating on Jamie but knew that was a ridiculous thought.

Then he felt bad about Sarah. She was a nice girl and fun to spend time with, but Ben was sure he wasn't going to be able to give her the kind of attention and appreciation she deserved.

He hated one-night stands and had only a few back in his college days. Once he heard the stories from his sisters about guys who had treated them poorly, he vowed to not be "one of them." He screwed up this time.

He credited his error partially to the alcohol but mostly the rebound effect. True, he was never really with Jamie but using one woman to get over another was a fairly common practice. Not one Ben was proud to have sunk to though.

Sarah stirred beside him. Ben caressed her arm, trying to decide how he was going to escape this situation without insulting her.

"Good morning," she mumbled, squeezing him across the chest.

"Good morning, yourself." They lay listening to the sounds of the cars going by on the street.

"Who's Jamie to you?" she asked sleepily.

Ben's hand paused mid-stroke and his heart raced.

She laughed. "Don't sweat it," she said. "It wasn't as if I couldn't tell you were drinking to forget." She snuggled in closer to him. "We all have our issues."

His hand resumed tracing the muscles of her forearm.

"She must be pretty special. You were talking to her in your sleep."

Ben sighed. "It's complicated."

"Most things worth having are."

"It won't work. She's married."

"Happily?"

It was an innocent question, but Ben wasn't sure how to respond. They usually avoided the topic of her husband. Ben sensed Jamie was unhappy but not miserable. He didn't get the impression Eddie was a total loser, but he wasn't very attentive. He certainly didn't give her the love she deserved.

"I don't know," he answered finally.

"Maybe you should ask her."

"And how exactly does that conversation start? 'If you aren't happily married, maybe you could break your wedding vows to hook up with me for a while? No promises though.' Doesn't sound very convincing."

"Not when you say it like that." Sarah sat up in bed and was not at all self-conscious when the sheet slipped away. "Have you told her how you feel?"

"No. I can't. I don't want to make her uncomfortable. What if her home life is perfectly fine, and I'm just wishing it was on the rocks? What a cruel thing to wish for. What kind of person wants a friend's marriage to break up? And to make matters worse, we work together. What if I bare my soul and it doesn't matter to her? It'll be awkward."

The fact that he was laying naked in a bed with an incredibly beautiful, and equally naked, woman, talking about another woman was surreal. A smile stole across his face, and he shook his head.

"I'm sorry. This is unfair to you," Ben said.

Sarah brushed away his apology. "Don't feel sorry for me. I got what I wanted."

Ben blushed as her eyes surveyed his body thoroughly. He chastised himself when he felt stirrings under the sheets. "Dammit, woman, have you no pity?"

She leaned in close to him and ran her fingers across his chest. "Not really."

Ben groaned in frustration as he fought with himself.

"Here's how I see it," she said. "I know where your heart is, but I'm not interested in your heart." Her hand slid down to his hip.

"You're currently unattached and have made no commitments to this married woman, Jamie." Her hand stroked his thigh and moved back up to where his interest was growing. "You are a free man, capable of making your own decisions. I'm a free woman, and I want your decision to be about the here and now. Allow me a little fun before you go off and flog yourself over a situation you can't change."

She stretched her body out to cover his, her bare breasts burning against his chest.

"Well, since you put it that way," Ben said, his resolve slipping. She did have a point. He wasn't committed to anyone, and he did need to move on from his infatuation with Jamie.

He tangled his fingers in her hair and pulled her face close to his for a deep kiss. Even as his hips began to get into rhythm with Sarah's movements, he saw Jamie again. He pushed the thought aside and focused on the moment, but he couldn't stop himself from wishing it was Jamie's body he was exploring.

The following week, Jamie emailed her report off to Steven at the home office and awaited his call. It came before lunch.

"Great job, Jamie. I sure picked the right person to figure this out. I wouldn't have been half as clever."

"Thank you. I will admit it was kind of fun to set the trap."

"Now you can go ahead and start the process of hiring a replacement. It's key position so it shouldn't be hard to fill. Especially for the salary we're offering," Steven said.

"Already started the paperwork," Jamie said.

"I know you've been gone a while already, but it would help me out if you would stay on a while longer and conduct sensitivity training. Perhaps we can avoid situations like this in the future."

Although anxious to get back to her own life, Jamie didn't feel she could let Steven down. They agreed she would stay in Virginia Beach until just before Thanksgiving.

She decided she would stop at her mom's house on her way back to D.C. She could use a little coddling from her mother.

While confident in her work performance, Jamie was still struggling with her self-confidence as a woman. She continually replayed the years of her marriage and tried to pick apart every little thing she might have done differently to save it.

Maybe if she had fed his ego a little more. Maybe if she had been more of a homemaker. Maybe she should have dressed sexier. She stopped there. No matter how hard she tried, she didn't think she could have given him the leather-look Eddie was aroused by. She could never have foreseen this turn of events.

To stop dwelling on the past, she dreamt of Ben—during the day and at night. Would she have a chance with him? Thoughts of him eased the pain over her divorce. She envisioned inviting him over for dinner and seducing him with candlelight and soft music. She'd wear something blue, his favorite color. It had to be low cut. Jamie still had a decent figure, and she was much more tone after months of working out. She planned her every move. Jamie wasn't sure she could keep him on script though. It hadn't worked out the way she planned last time. But now there was nothing holding them back.

Chapter 26

Jamie opened the kitchen door and was greeted with the scent of home. One of those things you don't know you've missed unless you've been gone awhile. She placed her purse on the counter and rolled her suitcase into the laundry room. The house was very quiet.

She'd only made it home once during her three-month absence. The neighbor boy had done a good job watching over her house and yard while she was away, and everything was in good order.

As she wandered into the bedroom, Jamie was relieved to note Eddie had come and gone, removing the last of his personal belongings. That was one less thing for her to deal with.

She finished her walk through the house and returned to the kitchen. Looking around at the boring walls, a thought struck her. She had always wanted to paint the kitchen green. Now that Eddie was gone, she could do it. Jamie smiled at the little things signaling her freedom.

She was full of energy and began pulling dirty clothes from her suitcase and tossing them into the washer. She set aside the things she would have to drop at the dry cleaners. The doorbell rang. Surprised, she went to answer it. Trina stood on the front step, presenting a pizza box. Jamie opened the door widely to her friend.

"Welcome home!" Trina said.

"Thanks," Jamie answered, taking the box and giving Trina a one-armed hug. "Come in. It's so great to see you."

Trina followed Jamie into the kitchen. Jamie put the box on the table and grabbed plates from the cupboard. Trina grabbed sodas from the near-empty refrigerator. "Glad I brought my own food. Your cupboards are bare, Old Mother Hubbard."

"I just walked in. Your timing's perfect."

They sat down to eat, and Trina launched into what was happening around the office. Jamie was dying to know how Ben was doing but didn't want to ask directly.

Eventually Trina offered the information herself. "Seems like Ben has a live-in," she announced, almost with too much cheer in her voice.

Jamie's heart stopped. Trying to sound casual, she asked, "What do you mean?"

"He's been spotted around town with a gorgeous blonde and others have commented on seeing an extra car parked in his driveway for a few weeks now."

Jamie felt Trina's gaze on her. This would be the perfect time for Jamie to open up to her about her feelings for Ben. Trina was giving her the opportunity.

Jamie felt sick. She finally had her chance, and it had come too late. While she was gone, she often thought about calling Ben but didn't know how to start the conversation. She was still embarrassed he didn't kiss her when she had so boldly demanded it.

She didn't feel she could just call him up and say, "Oh, by the way, my husband didn't want me anymore. Want to give it a shot?"

She still wasn't sure enough of herself to get involved in another relationship, but she had hoped, in time, Ben would give her a chance.

"How was Thanksgiving? Go anywhere special?" Jamie asked, changing the subject.

"My sisters were all tied up, so I had some friends over at my place. Believe it or not, we actually played board games after dinner."

Jamie almost choked on her pizza. "Really? Board games?"

"It was a family tradition in my house. We each got to pick a game, and everyone had to play."

"What a great tradition. I'll have to remember that one."

"I'm going to my oldest sister's for Christmas. My youngest sister and her boyfriend are going to join us, but my middle sister has to go to her new in-laws."

"It's great that most of you can be together," Jamie said wistfully.

"What about you? Did you go to your mom's for Thanksgiving?"

"I did. She put out a full spread although it was just the three of us, including Bob. Then we packaged up the leftovers and took them to her pastor's house. He was too busy to stop for dinner, and she always makes too much. I suspect she does it on purpose just so she can feed him. He's a great guy. We joined him at the homeless shelter where they volunteer and served meals. It was exhausting but rewarding."

"Where was Eddie? Didn't he go with you?"

Jamie squirmed a little in her seat. She still felt like a failure on that front and hadn't shared details of the breakup with anyone.

She picked up the empty plates and put them in the sink. While her back was turned, Jamie said, "Eddie and I split up."

"What? When?" Trina was caught off guard.

"The last straw was before I left for Virginia Beach. He moved out while I was gone." She turned to face Trina. She didn't know how she felt at that moment. A little relieved to finally have told someone other than her mom, she had to admit to herself.

"Why didn't you tell me?"

Jamie returned to her seat and dropped into it heavily. "I didn't tell anyone. I'm embarrassed."

"There's nothing to be embarrassed about. It happens all the time," Trina consoled.

"My parents split when I was young. I didn't think the same thing would happen to me." She shrugged. "At least we didn't have kids."

Trina reached across the table and patted Jamie's hand. "What happened?"

"I found out he was cheating." Jamie couldn't bear to share the details of walking in on him and his *partner* with Trina. She hadn't even told her mother that slice.

"*He* was cheating?" Trina asked with a little too much emphasis on the pronoun.

Jamie looked at her quizzically. "Yes 'he.' What did you expect?"

"Well, I just thought…" Trina trailed off, pulling back her hand.

"You thought…" Jamie prompted, her ire rising.

"…the way you were carrying on with Ben…"

Jamie stared at her incredulously. A hundred images flashed through her head. She must have been more obvious than she'd assumed.

She shook her head in disappointment. Then she took a deep breath and blew it out. "No," she responded. Jamie had to be fair. She had no reason to be mad at Trina for suspecting her. She did, after all, have feelings for Ben. It wasn't much of a leap to think she might have acted on them.

"Ben and I weren't having an affair—not a physical one anyway. We flirted a lot but never crossed the line." Jamie picked up her soda can and studied the writing without seeing it.

"He filled a void Eddie wasn't interested in filling." Jamie said. "He appreciated hanging with me, and that was enough for him. But I guess I couldn't expect it to be enough forever."

"What did Ben say when you told him?" Trina asked.

"I didn't tell him."

"What?" Trina said in disbelief. "You need to tell him."

"I can't. Not now. It would be weird. We never talked about my marriage before. I can't all of a sudden want to talk about it being over without looking pathetic."

"Don't be ridiculous. I'll tell him if you want. I can just mention it in passing."

"No, please. Don't do that. If he's with someone else now, I don't want to seem like I'm fishing. Besides, it's too soon for me to get involved with anyone. I just got divorced. I need time to get used to the idea. I'd hate to confuse him by chasing him on the rebound, only to discover I'm not ready to get involved again."

Trina looked at her friend.

"Promise me," Jamie insisted.

"I promise. But I think you're nuts."

Trina changed the conversation and tried to take Jamie's mind off Ben. They discussed other mutual acquaintances, and Jamie tried to follow the conversation, but only half-heartedly.

She filled Trina in on the tangled webs at the Virginia Beach office and the eventual outcome. She explained about the woman who had started the rumors and the fake Facebook page. An official announcement was not made as to the reason she was fired, but the word rapidly spread it was for unprofessional behavior. Everyone was able to guess the rest. It was fitting the same rumor mill that caused the problems would be the right venue to get the word out. Most people implied they didn't believe the initial stories. It was all too improbable.

After much coordination with the executives on the Facebook board, Scott's Facebook page disappeared from the web. A formal email from the Virginia Beach office manager had publicly cleared Scott Jansen from any wrongdoing and stated he had nothing to do with the posts. An apology was made to all affected, but no one denounced the real culprit.

Jamie had conducted the sensitivity training, and it had been well-received. Many women had approached her afterwards and thanked her. Even a few men acknowledged that it was long overdue. She had already talked to Steven about doing the same for the D.C. office.

"Damn. Your news trumps anything going on here. You're going to be bored by comparison," Trina said when Jamie finished.

"I'll take bored for a while. I need the break."

"Well, I'm here if you need to talk—about anything. Or if you need a wing-woman."

Jamie smiled. She could always count on Trina to be looking out for her social life.

Trina stood. "I need to get going. But let's plan on going out Friday."

They hugged in the doorway.

When Trina left, Jamie walked around the empty house, trying to get a feel for what it was going to be like for her living alone. She removed her wedding picture from the mantel and examined it.

Eddie looked so handsome in his black tuxedo and white rose boutonnière. She tried to read a hint of the future in his smile but didn't see it. She had no idea that "forever" meant until the next woman came along.

Chapter 27

The next morning, as Jamie prepared for work, she envisioned seeing Ben again. She couldn't blame him for having a girlfriend. After all, he was a very attractive, considerate man. Any girl would be lucky to be with him.

She spent a little extra time in front of the mirror applying makeup. She tried to tell herself it didn't have anything to do with Ben; it was part of the new "Jamie."

Butterflies filled her stomach as she drove toward the large, brick office complex. She remembered this feeling from her first day of work at Winkler and Stein less than a year ago. She was nervous then, too. Although not shy, Jamie could be reserved when she first met people. It was important to her to make a good impression.

But she didn't have anything to be nervous about today, she told herself. Maybe the butterflies were a sign of excitement simply because she had missed the work and the people and was looking forward to getting back into her routine. She pushed aside the thought that she missed one person in particular.

The first thing she noticed when she pulled into the parking lot was that Ben's car wasn't in his spot. Instead, there was a deep blue Mazda RX-8. Jamie couldn't help but wonder if this was part of his new life with the other woman. She felt a tug of jealousy.

She made her way down the hall with many well-wishers greeting her along the way. When she entered her office suite, Carolyn captured her in a bear hug, very happy to see her.

"Look at you!" Carolyn exclaimed, holding her at arms' length. "Don't they have food in Virginia Beach? You're too skinny. Don't you go losing any more weight! I won't be able to find you!"

After catching up for a few minutes, Jamie escaped to her office and booted up her computer. She was glad to be back.

She worked diligently over the next hour trying to catch up. She had been answering emails regularly while she was in Virginia Beach but there were never enough hours in the day to do everything.

She heard a quiet knock at her door and looked up to find Ben leaning on the doorframe, looking as great as ever. She smiled broadly and stood to greet him before she caught herself. He came around her desk and surprised her with a hug.

"I've missed you," he said before he released her.

Jamie felt the warmth of his body against hers and couldn't focus for a time.

"You didn't miss me?" he asked with a sparkle in his eye.

"Well, I did miss your stupid jokes once in a while," she admitted. "And I didn't have anyone to hang with on Fridays."

Ben laughed.

"I planned my return today just to attend First Friday and catch up with everyone. Are you going?" Jamie asked casually.

"Not this week," Ben said apologetically. "I already have plans. If I had known you'd be back, I would've blocked the evening for you."

Jamie tried to hide her disappointment.

"But why would I expect you would tell me you were coming back when you didn't even tell me you were leaving?" Ben threw at her.

Jamie felt the jab. "Yeah, I deserved that," she said.

Ben let it slide. "You look great," he said. "Did you live at the gym?"

Jamie blushed, glad he noticed. "There wasn't much else to do. Too cold in the fall to go to the beach. No one to drink with."

"Well, we'll make up for that."

Jamie hoped he was right.

First Friday wasn't the same without Ben at her table. She missed him even though she had seen him at work that morning. He never mentioned a girlfriend, but then, Jamie never mentioned her break-up with Eddie. It would be awkward to bring it up at work, and besides, they never talked about him before.

Trina slid into the booth across from to Jamie, passing her a beer. "How's it going?"

"It's good to be back."

Trina searched the room. "Where's Ben?"

Jamie shrugged. "Don't know. Said he had other plans tonight."

"The other woman? I wonder where she came from. No one new at work."

"People meet at other places than work."

"Yeah, but when?"

Jamie wasn't interested in this topic. "Thanks for the beer, but I'm more tired than I thought. Finish up for me, will you?"

She said goodbye to the gang and headed toward her car. Without intending to, her car started the route to Ben's home. She had been there once before with Trina for a party. It was in a quiet neighborhood not too far from the office and about equidistant from the Liberty Tavern. Jamie listened to the radio as she drove. Every song was a love song—getting together or breaking up. She turned the radio off and drove in silence.

Pulling up in front of his house, she parked on the street. She sat in the car trying to get up her nerve to knock on the door. Just as she was about to open her car door, headlights flashed in her rearview mirror and she froze. The car turned into Ben's driveway and parked. A slim figure got out of the car. Jamie couldn't make out features in the dark, but from the way she walked on the slippery sidewalk, she was definitely female.

The woman walked up the pathway, and Ben opened the front door before she had a chance to ring the bell. Jamie couldn't hear their words but sat frozen as Ben wrapped the young lady in his arms and led her inside.

As the door closed, Jamie felt something inside her die. She sat slumped at the steering wheel and cried silently. A few moments passed before she pulled herself together and wiped her eyes. She took a few deep breaths. What did she expect? There was no reason for Ben to wait for her. She put the car in gear and drove home.

On Monday, Ben stuck his head in Jamie's office.

"How was First Friday? Everything you remembered?"

Jamie looked up from her paperwork. "It was fine."

"That's it? Fine? Bet everyone was happy to see you."

"Ben, I appreciate the visit, but I'm swamped. Can we catch up later?"

A little stung, Ben put his hand over his heart. "I know when I'm not wanted. Maybe lunch?"

Jamie shrugged and went back to her work.

He backed out of her office. Ben could tell Jamie was upset with him but couldn't figure out why. He would have loved to be at the Liberty Tavern on Friday but couldn't be expected to drop everything for her. He did have his own life.

During the staff meeting, Jamie wouldn't even make eye contact with him. She had her head down writing in her notebook. Ben couldn't imagine anything Steven was saying was all that interesting.

He looked for her after the meeting, but she had ducked out. He couldn't figure out what had changed between them since she left for Virginia Beach. Maybe he was making her uncomfortable. They had gotten quite close and that couldn't be all right with her husband.

By Wednesday, Ben couldn't stand the cold shoulder any longer. He decided to try to make nice with Jamie.

Jamie was seated at her desk when Ben knocked on her door. He held a yellow rose around the door frame while shielding his body.

"Come in," Jamie said. "I don't bite."

Ben entered the room and handed her the rose. "Truce?"

"I didn't know we were at war," Jamie said.

"It feels like it," Ben said. "We hardly talk anymore."

Jamie glanced at her computer screen. "I'm just busy since I've been back," she said. "Things will calm down."

Ben took that as a hint to leave. "Are you going to the Christmas party?" he asked, trying to sound nonchalant.

She glanced up at him with a strange expression Ben couldn't read. "I doubt it. I haven't given it much thought."

Ben wasn't sure if he was relieved or not. He had already purchased his tickets, but he didn't want to spend the evening watching Jamie dance with her husband.

After Ben left, Jamie inhaled the rose's scent. It was lovely. She considered the Christmas party. She had been looking forward to dressing up and spending the evening with her friends—and maybe dazzling Ben. That was before she saw Ben with his girlfriend. She dropped the rose in the trash and turned back to the computer.

Chapter 28

"What do you mean you don't want to go to the party? You have to go." Trina worked hard to convince Jamie as they finished eating dinner later that night. "It's a blast. The top dogs go the extra mile to make it special. And the food is always the best."

Jamie still hesitated. Since she started working here, she had heard about the great Christmas parties thrown by Winkler and Stein, and after seeing their off-site, she could only imagine what they would do. Folks had been talking about it all week. How could she explain to Trina she wasn't ready to see Ben with someone else?

"I tell you what," Trina said, "let's book rooms at the hotel for that night. We'll spend the day of the party getting the spa treatment—massage, hair, nails—the works. Let's make it a coming out party since your divorce."

Under the constant pressure from Trina, Jamie was cracking. She could use some pampering. A smile crept over her face. She knew she cleaned up pretty well. Perhaps this was a chance to show Ben what he was missing. She gave in. "Okay. Let's do it."

She decided to go all out. If this was her chance to be noticed, she would do it right.

It took her days to find just the right dress. When she was married to Eddie, she would never have considered spending that kind of money on a dress she would probably wear only once. But she reminded herself, she was no longer married to Eddie. She handed the dress to a salesgirl to ring up.

It was midnight blue with sequins to add a little sparkle when she moved. The hem line was high on her thigh. The black shoes with stiletto heels took some practice walking in, but Jamie would wear them around the house for a few days prior to the party, just to be sure.

As the party drew closer, Jamie got more and more excited…and a little nervous. She didn't want to look foolish, so out of place playing dress up. Trina reassured her and focused her mind on the dancing and the band. They didn't mention Ben at all.

Christmas lights were strung in the trees lining the streets. Jamie knew the twinkling white stars would make even the older parts of the city look beautiful after dark.

She pulled up in front of the Gaylord National Resort on the bank of the Potomac River in Oxon Hill, Maryland. She looked around at the beautiful new buildings bordering the hotel. National Harbor was still growing with many restaurants and shops. Through the naked trees, she could see the yachts of the boat club bobbing in the water. She allowed the valet to take her bags from her trunk. She handed over her keys and walked to the front desk.

The lobby was huge with a long counter running most of the length. Jamie was greeted and given her room key. The valet offered to take her bags to her room while she picked up her complimentary drink at the wine bar. He encouraged her to look around and take her time.

Jamie heeded his advice and strolled toward the sound of music being played on the other side of the greenery. She was surprised to see a live jazz ensemble playing softly while a few guests listened and visited with each other. She accepted a wine glass off a tray presented by a gentleman in a white jacket. *This is a very classy place indeed*, she thought.

She took her wine and did some window shopping at the many stores inside the hotel. A flash of movement in the distance caught her eye, and she headed down the escalator to explore. A large fountain shot water high into the air in time with music playing over a speaker. Colored lights added to the show, and it was mesmerizing. As Jamie watched, she found herself relaxing and took another sip from her glass.

"There you are," Trina said. "I was wondering when you'd get here. Can you believe this place?"

Jamie turned to greet her friend with a hug, careful not to spill her drink. "It's gorgeous. I feel like we're in a fairy tale."

"I told you Winkler does it right. They set aside a whole block of rooms for folks so they wouldn't drink and drive. Even subsidized some of the cost to make it more attractive."

"Works for me," Jamie said. Trina had reserved one room because her boyfriend Neil was meeting her at the party, and Jamie took another.

"Let's get some lunch. This wine is going to my head already," Trina said taking Jamie's arm.

After lunch, Trina and Jamie reported to the spa for their massage and facial appointments. They were given white fluffy bathrobes to change into and cool glasses of water while they waited in the low light of the spa receiving area. Within five minutes, two attendants came and swept them off to separate rooms for their massages.

Two hours later they rejoined, faces glowing from the apricot scrubs. They were ushered into high seats in front of bubbling tubs of water for their feet. Someone took their drink orders as they mulled over the right color of nail polish.

They were served wine and cheese while professional women scoured their feet and pretended not to be able to overhear their conversation.

"I'm in heaven," Jamie said as the young lady massaged her feet. "I've been practicing in the high heels and my feet aren't used to the abuse. Give me flats and sneakers any day."

Trina laughed, her head back and eyes closed, enjoying the pedicure herself. "Wait until the manicure."

"I've never had one before."

Trina's eyes flew open. "What rock have you been living under?"

"It was never in the budget."

"Well, now you are writing your own budget. Pampering yourself once in a while must be on it."

When the ladies started work on her hands, Jamie was surprised. She had thought it was just getting your nails painted. She never realized it included a hand massage, moisturizing lotions, and so many layers of polish. This was pampering at its best.

While their nails dried, Trina and Jamie were directed into the hair salon. The stylist held up various pictures for the women to choose from. They consulted each other and fussed back and forth over their decision, finally allowing the stylist to make the choice.

Last but not least, two women arrived wheeling a tray resembling a paint palette. Jamie noticed the trays weren't the same, each one having been selected to complement

Jamie's and Trina's complexions. Hours after they had entered the spa, their transformation was complete. They were allowed to slip back into their street clothes, very carefully, so as not to mess their hair or nails. They were given a square of chocolate, wished a pleasant evening, and were released back into the hustle and bustle of the hotel lobby.

The ladies parted in high spirits, agreeing to meet downstairs in an hour for the party.

Jamie paced around her room, trying to work off the nervous energy. She didn't want to get dressed too soon and then sit around waiting. Instead she grabbed lotion from the gift basket in her room. She sat on the edge of the bed and took her time applying it to her legs and arms. All the working out had paid off. Her legs were nice and firm. Her arms were well defined. Overall, she felt great.

She decided it was time to get dressed. She slipped the slinky dress over her head, careful to not mess up her hair. It fit perfectly, outlining her curves and dipping low enough to show off her cleavage.

The added height of her heels accentuated her calf muscles. She took a long look in the full-length mirror and smiled.

Self-consciously, Jamie entered the ballroom and looked around. Trina was instantly at her side with two other co-workers. Trina gave her a reassuring squeeze. "You look dynamite."

They exchanged comments on hair, outfits, and the beautiful decorations. Jamie tried to scan the crowd without making it too obvious.

"Jamie, you look lovely." Jamie turned to greet her boss Steven. He handed her a glass of white wine and took her by the elbow to guide her further into the room. "I want you to meet someone."

He led her to a small group. As they approached, a handsome gentleman must have just delivered the punch line because the gathering broke into laughter.

"Jon, I'd like you to meet Jamie," Steven said presenting Jamie. "Jamie, this is Jon Waters. He's from the Chicago office. He just can't pass up a good party."

Jon took Jamie's offered hand. "Nice handshake. That says a lot about a woman," Jon said.

"And about a man," Jamie replied as she dropped his hand and smiled at the others. She knew them all by name, but they didn't run in the same circles. Most were years younger than she was.

"Absolutely," Jon recovered. "So, Jamie, where do you work?"

As Jamie went through the first-meeting drill, the others drifted away, leaving the two alone.

Soon Jamie found herself relaxing and laughing along with Jon's stories. When the announcement was made to be seated for dinner, Jamie accepted Jon's arm as he escorted her to a table.

"Are you kidding me?" Ben muttered to himself when he spotted Jamie across the ballroom and instantly felt a familiar stirring. He thought he had his feelings under control but seeing her now proved how wrong he was. She was gorgeous. Her long legs were emphasized by high heels he knew she hated.

"Ben, can I buy you a drink?" Jason Henderson was at his right elbow. He followed Ben's gaze. "Who's Jamie talking to? Wow! She looks great."

Jamie had decided to come after all, along with Eddie. He wasn't anything like Ben had expected. Ben turned away. "Let's get that drink."

At the bar, Jason and Ben were joined by a good looking blonde. She kissed Ben on the cheek, and he turned with a smile. "You made it!" Ben gave her a hug. "Jason, this is Ginger. Ginger, stay away from this guy."

Jason shook Ginger's hand. "Nice to meet you finally."

"Nice to meet you, Jason."

Ben ordered a glass of wine for Ginger and a gin and tonic for himself.

The call for dinner was announced and Jason, Ben, and Ginger made their way to a table.

Chapter 29

Ben pulled out Ginger's chair for her and took his seat. He was annoyed with himself when he selected a seat facing the table where Jamie and her husband sat. He didn't want to watch them but couldn't bring himself to move either. He nursed his third gin and tonic. He risked a glance at Jamie's table, but she was busy laughing at another comment made by her escort.

He felt sophomoric and tried to redirect his attention to Ginger and the conversation around him.

Dinner ended and Steven got up to make a few announcements. He kept it short, and the band started the evening of dancing.

Ben sat stewing as he watched Jamie's husband escort her to the dance floor. He didn't object when Jason asked Ginger to dance. She hit him on the shoulder as she passed. Ben headed back to the bar.

Trina's date broke in on Jamie and Jon as they danced and whisked Jamie away.

"Thanks," Jamie whispered. "I don't think I could keep up the small talk much longer."

"Trina caught your cry for help and sent me in for the rescue," Neil laughed as he danced her closer to the bar and a means of escape. They joined Trina at the bar, and she handed Jamie a drink. Jamie took a grateful gulp and a seat.

Neil slipped his arm around Trina, and Jamie was reminded again of how lucky she was to have such good friends. She took another sip and scoured the crowd. Ben was at the other end of the bar, soon joined by his blonde. They looked happy. Jamie's mood turned, and she ordered another round.

"Slow down, girl, you didn't eat much," Trina cautioned.

"I'm not driving, remember?" Jamie lifted her glass in a salute. Trina exchanged a glance with Neil.

Ben caught sight of Jamie. She hadn't talked to him all night. Where was Eddie, he wondered? He spotted him on the floor, dancing very close to another woman. He couldn't believe that didn't bother Jamie, but she didn't seem to be paying him any attention. Just as Ben got up the courage to approach Jamie, another man led her to the dance floor.

When the song slowed down, Jamie excused herself back to a table by the bar. Trina and Neil were dancing, and Jamie watched them. She started when Ben spoke.

"You look thirsty," he said as he passed a drink to her and took a seat.

Jamie smiled in acknowledgment. She sipped the gin and tonic and laughed. "Most guys would have brought wine," she said.

"Most guys don't know you."

She took another drink as Ben watched the redness color her cheeks.

"You look absolutely fabulous," he said.

"Thanks. You look mighty nice yourself." She let her eyes linger on his.

Ben broke eye contact first. "So, how's it going?" he asked. "Is Eddie enjoying the party?"

"Eddie?" Jamie looked confused. "Eddie isn't here," she said.

"Oh, I thought—" Ben stopped. Relief swept over him—but then confusion. Who was the guy she was sitting with at dinner?

Jamie was eying him.

Ben looked up and saw Ginger motioning him over. He didn't want to leave Jamie, but Ginger was insistent. "Wait here. There's someone I want you to meet," Ben told Jamie.

She followed his movement across the room and saw him walk right up to *her*. Jamie had no intention of waiting around for him. She'd go find someone else to entertain her. She was tired of waiting on men. And she certainly didn't want to meet his girlfriend.

Jamie put her hand on the man's shoulder and leaned in to whisper something. They both laughed, and Jamie ran her hand down his arm. She glanced up to see Ben looking in her direction.

Ben seethed with jealousy. From across the bar he was riveted to this spectacle like an accident scene. When he had returned to the table with Ginger, Jamie was gone. Now she was chatting up someone else at the bar. When the man pressed closer to Jamie, Ben couldn't take it anymore. He pushed his way through the crowd to where they stood.

Ben took Jamie's arm. "Time to go."

Jamie pushed his hand away. "I'm not going anywhere. I'm staying here. This nice gentleman just bought me a drink," she said, patting his arm.

"You've had enough to drink," Ben insisted.

"Listen to her. She says she wants to stay," the man said, slurring his words.

Ben felt a hand on his arm, "Come on, Ben. Don't do this," Ginger said.

"Yeah, Ben, I can take care of myself," Jamie said.

Ginger pulled on his arm and walked him away from the scene.

"That's bad news," Ben snarled.

"I understand you're concerned, but they're only having a drink." She drew him to the dance floor. "You haven't danced with me all night. I love this song."

Ben fought to control his jealousy and to focus on Ginger. She made silly dance moves to make Ben smile, and he started to loosen up. When the slow music started, Jason cut in and pushed Ben to the sidelines. Ben waved as he walked outside to cool down.

He stood under the hotel awning but away from the smokers' area. The cold air was refreshing after the heat generated on the dance floor. Off to his right, Ben heard a rustling. He looked into the shadows but couldn't make out anything.

"Stop it," he heard faintly.

He recognized the voice and his heart jumped.

"You son of a bitch!" accompanied by a loud slap.

"Whadda you do that for?" a male voice slurred. "I just wanted to look."

"I said I want to go back inside. I feel better now."

"Just stay out a little longer," the voice pleaded.

"Let me go!"

Adrenaline seized him as he ran outside the circle of light and toward the parking lot on the side of the hotel.

"C'mon, you little bitch. Let me look."

Ben moved blindly in the darkness as his eyes adjusted. His ears tuned in to the sounds beyond his vision. He heard a struggle and moved in that direction. As his eyes became accustomed, he could make out figures in the distance. His heart was in his throat as he rushed toward the scene.

"You're a little tease, Miss High and Mighty." Ben heard the deep voice say through gritted teeth. "Not so impressed with yourself now, are you?"

Some man Ben didn't recognize had his arms locked around Jamie's back in a bear hug as she fought to free herself. He was one hundred pounds heavier than she was and very determined.

"Hey!" Ben yelled as approached the scene at a full sprint.

The man looked up in surprise, and Jamie took the opportunity to bring her knee up sharply into his groin. As the man released her and doubled over, she chopped him on the back of the neck and he hit the ground face first.

Ben was frozen. The thought of Jamie in danger had charged all his emotions and prepared him for a fight. Now the object of his hatred lay on a heap in the dirty snow, and there was nothing for him to do.

Jamie wiped her hands together and stepped unsteadily toward Ben in her heels. He reached out to take her in his arms, but she walked past him without stopping.

"Jamie…" Ben followed her. "Are you okay?"

From the dark, the man on the ground groaned and then began retching.

"I'm fine. Why wouldn't I be?" She continued unsteadily toward the hotel entrance.

Ben could hear her voice shaking. He reached to take her arm, and she shook his hand away.

"That was pretty amazing," he said, trying to get her to open up to him. "Glad I never made you mad."

She didn't answer. Her steps slowed and became halted.

Ben persisted in his attempt to reach her. "Will you teach me those moves? I could use them walking home late at night." He laughed but it was hollow-sounding.

Jamie slowed down and stumbled as the adrenaline rush subsided. She started shaking, and Ben was sure it wasn't only from the cold. He took off his jacket and put it around her shoulders. They had almost reached the main doors to the hotel.

"Come on, Jamie. I'll give you a ride home." Ben gently but firmly put his arm around her shoulders. This time she didn't resist his touch.

"No. I'm fine."

"Jamie, you aren't fine. You're awesome!"

She gave him a strange look.

"You handled yourself well, but that was still a shitty experience. I can't believe you're still standing. I'd be a pile of goo right now."

She straightened her back and focused on the music coming from the ballroom. "I need a drink."

Ben saw the resolution in her stance but couldn't understand it. She had a terrific shock. Why wouldn't she let him help? They had been friends for almost a year. They had talked about all kinds of things. Now it was as if she was intentionally shutting him out. It scared him.

He knew she had a fright, and the realization of what could have happened was going to hit her soon. She shouldn't be alone when it happened.

Jamie looked into Ben's eyes and saw concern. She wanted to melt into his arms and forget everything. She was scared and trying to maintain control. Then she remembered he had other priorities. His blonde was waiting for him. The thought bolstered her courage. She didn't want to seem vulnerable or needy. She didn't want to show him that he meant anything to her.

"Please let me give you a ride home," he said again as he tried to steer her toward the parking lot.

"No, thank you. I have a room." Jamie shrugged him off and walked toward the sliding glass doors. She was feeling a little nauseous and certainly didn't want to be sick in front of Ben. The episode in the yard was bad enough. She was kicking herself for even allowing herself to become so vulnerable. She knew better. She hadn't noticed the creep following her until it was too late. She had just needed to get away from Ben and his girlfriend. It never occurred to her she wouldn't be safe outside such a fancy hotel.

Ben followed close at her heels, trying to be helpful. "Let me at least walk you to your room," he said.

Jamie was confused. She was scared and wanted nothing more to fall into Ben's arms for shelter, but she didn't want to be helpless in front of him again.

"I don't need you to protect me," she said, but her legs betrayed her as she stumbled against him. Instantly she felt the familiar spark she had been avoiding. She was physically drawn to him like a magnet.

"You proved you don't need me," he said watching her face. "But do you want me?"

What the hell, she thought. She let her eyes travel up and down his body. She was tired of being the one in reaction mode, always waiting for something to happen. She wanted to call the shots. The alcohol was making her more forward than usual. Aloud she said, "I'm open to suggestions."

His smile was warm and roguish. Jamie was glad to sense the attraction went both ways.

As they reached the elevator, Ginger and Jason approached them. Ginger spotted Jamie wearing Ben's coat and raised a questioning eyebrow at Ben. "Ben, Jason's going to give me a ride home if that's okay," she asked.

"I warned you about him," Ben said with a grin. "You're taking your life into your hands."

Before she had a chance to escape, Ben's hold on her arm tightened. He introduced the couple.

"Jamie, you know Jason from the office." Jamie nodded and forced a smile. "This is Ginger, my sister. She's been visiting from New York."

Jamie's knees felt weak. His sister? She held out her hand, and Ginger took it warmly.

"Ben has told me a lot about you," Ginger said. She turned to Ben. "I hope you don't mind that I'm running off on you. I'm tired of dancing."

Ben gave her a kiss on the cheek. "Thanks for coming with me," he said. He shook Jason's hand and added, "I'll kill you if she gets hurt."

Ginger hit Ben playfully, and they walked away.

Jamie was still reeling from the realization that Ben didn't have a date. He had a sister!

Chapter 30

Jamie allowed Ben to lead her into the elevator. She pushed the button to her floor in silence. Ben released her arm but stood close to her. Jamie could feel the heat from him and craved more.

They walked unhurriedly down the hall. Ben took her key card, opening the door to her room. "Do you want to come in?" she asked almost shyly.

"I don't think it would be a good idea," Ben objected.

"Come on. We hardly talk anymore. I've missed you."

Ben didn't argue. He came in and closed the door. She tossed his suit jacket on the couch and excused herself to go to the bathroom. When she came out, she had removed her shoes.

"Sorry, I wore them as long as I could," Jamie said. She took a seat on the couch and pulled her feet under her.

"I know what you mean," he said, tossing his tie on his jacket. Ben sat in the matching armchair, kicked off his shoes, and put his feet up on the coffee table. Their conversation started out stilted but gradually fell back into their usual rhythm. Jamie sobered as she told Ben about Jon and how the conversation kept circling around back around to his triumphs on the college football team.

"You should have asked him to teach you how to play," Ben said. "After he saw you throw, he would have left you alone." They laughed together, and it felt like it used to be.

Jamie just wanted to touch him—simply to make contact. It didn't have to be sexual. She told herself this over and over again, but she knew the alcohol lowered her guard. She had a hard time telling herself no.

She watched Ben as he talked. She was listening but another part of her craved closeness. She loved his eyes. The way he looked at her made her feel special.

She got up to get a glass of water. He watched her move and she felt self-conscious. She finished her drink and moved innocently behind his chair. Before she could talk herself out of it, she reached out to stroke his neck. After first contact, she became braver. With both hands, she began to knead his shoulders. He exhaled in delight. Jamie felt the heat rise in her.

It's innocent, she told herself as she slid her hands under the collar of his shirt to feel her skin on his.

Jamie's body wasn't fooled. She leaned into him, the desire for touch more intense. As she played her hands over his shoulders and down his back, she felt the heat grow between her legs. Her thoughts raced, but she tried to focus on the moment. He felt so good. Touching him was a relief. She had held back for so long.

He rested back against her body; his eyes closed. She wasn't sure what he was thinking, but he was enjoying himself. She smiled. Her hands moved around to his chest, and she slid her hands inside his shirt. Unfastening a few buttons gave her hands more freedom.

Ben shifted in his seat. Apparently, she wasn't the only one who had gone beyond innocent thoughts. As she continued to work, Ben reached back to touch her. Jamie felt weak. His hand played along her arm, and she redoubled her efforts to stay focused.

With a sigh, Ben took her hand and pulled Jamie around the chair to face him. She dropped down to her knees so their faces were inches apart. He stroked her face with the back of his right hand and looked into her eyes. There was a question in the air. Jamie was screaming the answer back to him inside her head. She longed for his kiss.

"My turn," he said. He firmly placed his hands on her shoulders and turned her around. She sat on the floor in front of him, more than a little frustrated. He brushed the hair off her neck, sending electricity through her body. When she felt the zipper slide down her dress, she shuddered. His warm hands caressed her shoulders. The massage was wonderful, but his touch was liable to send her over the edge. She tried to relax but the sexual tension was too strong. He sighed and his hands rested in place. She wanted to know what was going through his mind.

Jamie turned her head to the side so her cheek brushed his left hand. This time it was more than a sigh that escaped his lips. Jamie reached up and cautiously took his hand. He didn't resist. She brushed her lips against his fingers. She was beyond caring about anything but the feel of him. Opening his hand, she kissed his palm. Her tongue darted out to taste him. As she played her tongue over the tip of his thumb, his right hand tightened on her shoulder. Her lips parted and she became more aggressive in her intent. Ben moaned this time and pulled his hand back.

Jamie was disappointed but undeterred. Ben began rubbing her shoulders again. This time she reached up to him, taking his hands in hers, and guided them downward. His hand cupped over her breasts, hesitantly at first but then with more confidence. Jamie leaned back so her head rested on his chest. He slipped his hands inside her dress, and the warmth of her skin caught him on fire. His hands were gentle and patient.

When Jamie could stand it no longer, she rose to her knees and turned to kneel in front of him again. This time she would not be put off. She stared intently into his eyes as she allowed her dress to slide from her shoulders and off her arms. The dark blue lace of her filmy bra was a striking contrast against her pale skin. Ben took in the sight of her with appreciation.

He took her face in his hands and pulled her face closer. Jamie was trembling with excitement. His lips brushed hers, so softly. His tongue darted out, searching, probing. She couldn't stand it any longer. Her hands reached behind his head, pulling him closer. Her mouth hungrily closed on his; her tongue reaching for his—touching then pulling away. His lips were soft but demanding. He teased and satisfied. She had never been kissed like this and wanted it to go on forever.

Ben slid his hands down her body, his fingers lightly tracing the lace on her bra. Her nipples hardened at his touch. Too slowly for Jamie, Ben reached the clasp on the front of her bra. He pulled away from their kiss to look into Jamie's face. He watched her eyes for the permission he sought. She covered his hands with hers and moved them away. Ben's eyes flashed disappointment. Jamie continued to watch his face as she herself unclasped the bra, allowing her breasts to fall free. Ben's eyes no longer showed disappointment but a fiery look of passion.

Ben ran his thumbs over the erect nipples and was rewarded with a sharp intake of breath from Jamie. Her eyes closed and her head tilted as she arched her back. Ben pulled her closer and kissed her exposed neck.

Jamie's hands frantically worked at the buttons on his shirt. She could feel his heart beating fast, matching the rhythm of her own. Again, his mouth found hers. How he could kiss so tenderly but with so much passion was a mystery to her. It made her want him even more.

She gave up on the buttons in frustration, and Ben laughed under his breath. He sat back and finished the job she had started, pulling his shirt off. Her eyes took in the muscles on his chest and continued down to his flat stomach. The bulge in his slacks was begging for attention, and Jamie was more than happy to oblige. She ran her hands over his chest, enjoying the feel of the fine hairs, every sense heightened. She leaned in to run her tongue over his right nipple. Ever so tenderly, she let her lips linger there and she stroked with her tongue. His response was gratifying.

Her hands continued downward until they rested on his hips, thumbs stroking the tightness of the fabric in the center. She glanced to his face. His eyes were closed. Rising up, she kissed his neck, behind his ear, and found her way back to his mouth. She had less trouble with the zipper than she had with buttons and quickly released him. She could feel him trembling now.

He held her face between his palms again and controlled the kiss while she continued to explore. She slid her hands inside the waistband of his shorts, running her fingers back and forth but just out of reach of her intended target. When her finger finally made contact, Ben's kiss froze as his concentration was focused elsewhere. Jamie took the opportunity to slip out of his grasp and kiss her way down his chest. All the while, her fingers continued to tease.

Ben wrapped his fingers in her hair and leaned back into the chair. Jamie persisted in kissing his stomach while her hands moved back to his hips, determined to remove the material obstruction. Ben raised his hips to accommodate and Jamie slid his slacks and shorts off in the same motion. She rocked back on her knees to pull them off fully. Ben watched her face as she took in the sight of his nakedness. It took all her will power not to pull him to her at that moment. She wanted him desperately, but she wanted this to last.

Again, she kissed his chest, then his stomach. Her hair brushed against his groin and his hardness reached out for her. She made her way lower and her tongue caught the wetness that escaped from him. His hands were on her shoulders, kneading with the intensity building within him. Her tongue outlined the head of his manhood, licking teasingly around the rim. She circled his tip one last time with her tongue and took him into her mouth, dying to taste him. He responded with a moan. His fingers were trapped in her hair again, holding her in place but not against her will. She closed her lips around his shaft and let her teeth gently graze his skin. She moved up and down in a sensual motion; all the while Ben moved with her.

Her hands went to work now, stroking the inside of his thighs and finding their way into the play. She cupped him with one hand and gently squeezed. He pushed harder into her mouth, and she opened wider to accommodate.

"Jamie, stop," Ben said breathlessly. "Really, stop." He eased her away and pulled her up. Jamie was confused, sure she had done something wrong. Her concern must have been evident on her face because he smiled broadly and kissed her with growing passion. As they kissed, Ben worked his way out of the chair and pushed Jamie onto her back. Somehow, he never stopped kissing her and Jamie was wild with longing. When Ben sat up, Jamie tried to catch her breath. He was on his knees in front of her, working her dress over her hips and off. Her blue lace panties matched the bra that had been dispensed with earlier.

Ben ran his hands over the outside of her thighs, from her hips to her knees. Jamie shuddered and reached for Ben. He refused to allow her to pull him closer. With open palms, Ben massaged the inside of her thighs, spreading her legs. Jamie didn't resist. She was more than ready.

Ben leaned over Jamie, kissing his way up her thighs. Jamie squirmed in sexual expectancy. She needed to feel him inside her. She grasped his head and ran her fingers through his hair. His hot breath reached her mound and mingled with her wetness. The lace of her panties was no protection for the intensity of Ben's resolve. Using his hands to raise her hips off the ground, Ben peeled her panties away with his teeth.

There was a raging inferno inside of Jamie now. She didn't think she could wait any longer. She needed to feel him inside her now! She tried to pull Ben up beside her but there was no rushing him. He took his time, kissing his way up her body. Jamie was not beyond begging and opened her mouth to admit it when Ben took her right breast in his mouth. She couldn't speak. His tongue darted teasingly as his hand continued its exploration between her legs.

He allowed Jamie to pull his head up to her mouth. She kissed him deeply, sharing her passion.

He pulled away breathless and rested on one elbow beside Jamie. He ran his fingers over her naked body, taking it all in with his eyes.

"Why do you insist on torturing me?" Jamie asked exasperated.

Ben smiled sadly. "I want to give you plenty of time to change your mind. I don't want you to be sorry."

"Are you joking?"

"This is a serious step. Once I've had you, I don't think I'll be able to get enough."

"I don't see that as a problem," she answered.

Ben didn't need any more encouragement. He kissed fervently and covered her body with his.

Chapter 31

Lying together on the floor, bodies drenched in sweat but satisfied, Ben took in a deep breath. Jamie rolled on her side and looked at him. He traced the line of her jaw with his fingertips.

"That was the best Christmas present I ever received," he said gazing into her eyes. "Are you okay?"

"Ummm," she replied with a smile she didn't think would ever recede. Her hand rubbed his chest and teased his nipple.

"Hold that thought," he said, releasing himself from her arms. He stood, heading for the bathroom. Jamie watched him go and took the opportunity to admire his naked backside.

"Damn," she said in appreciation. She was very happy.

She heard the water running in the tub and felt herself drifting off to sleep. Before long, she felt Ben's gentle hands take hers, and he helped her to her feet. He guided her into the steamy bathroom where the flickering candlelight bounced like stars off the many mirrors. No words were exchanged as he kissed her before helping her step into the warm, bubble bath.

Jamie sank into the water with a sigh. It felt wonderful and luxurious. She couldn't remember the last time she had soaked in a tub. Now Ben was stepping in, and she leaned forward to give him room behind her. He wrapped his legs around her hips, and she was once again pleasantly surprised how nicely and naturally they fit together.

She leaned back, placing her head on his chest. He kneaded her shoulders, and she sighed.

"Where did you find the candles?" she asked with her eyes closed, focusing on his touch.

"Under the sink, along with the bubble bath. You must have gotten a surprise upgrade with your suite. Unless of course you were expecting someone," Ben's voice trailed off.

Jamie didn't answer as his hands slid to cup her breasts. His thumbs played over her nipples, and they rose in response. She could feel him pressing into the small of her back, and she exerted a little extra pressure to acknowledge his attention.

"This is more than I could have hoped for," she said, enjoying his hands exploring her body. "You have wonderful hands."

They slipped down to her waist and rested on her hip bones. "You need to eat more," he said. "You're getting bony."

"You need to search out the softer parts," she said, moving his hands inward to touch her curls.

"Like this?" he asked.

"Definitely." She rocked her hips in response to his rhythm.

Ben kissed her neck and let his tongue run lightly over her ear. He paused in his ministrations. She could hear him trying to control his breathing. "Sorry, my intent was to relax you. I didn't have a hidden agenda."

"I get very relaxed after orgasm," Jamie said matter-of-factly. Using the sides of the tub, careful not to knock over the candles on the edge, she pushed herself up. As she lowered herself to rest on Ben's hips, he glided smoothly inside her, and once again they began moving together in a way that came natural to them.

Jamie was enthralled by the thought of this gorgeous man touching her, and she felt something she hadn't felt in years—love.

The water was getting cold, and most the candles had gone out when splashed with water from the tub. Ben extinguished the others, and they made their way back to the bed.

Ben wrapped his arms around Jamie and held her for warmth and comfort. She spooned into him and hugged his arms. As she felt him drifting off to sleep, she was overwhelmed with a feeling of contentment and hope for the future.

"I love you," she whispered.

Ben squeezed her and murmured through his sleep, "I love you too."

Ben woke early the next morning and smiled at Jamie's sleeping form. Although her back was turned to him, she was spooned into his arms and had a peaceful smile on her face. Ben couldn't believe this beautiful woman spent the night with him. And what a night! Ben felt stirrings at the memory but decided to let Jamie sleep a little longer. He slipped out of the bed and grabbed his clothes. Noiselessly, he dressed in the bathroom. He wasn't sure what the next step would be. He knew Jamie had to go back to her husband but didn't know if he was going to be able to let her go without a fight.

He pondered his next move as he slipped softly out the hotel door in search of coffee and breakfast for Jamie. As he crossed the lobby, he heard someone call his name.

"Ben? I thought that was you."

Ben turned to face his boss. "Morning, Steven."

"Glad you had enough sense to stay the night rather than drive after drinking. I'd hate for a great night to end in an accident."

"Of course." Ben looked down at his wrinkled suit. "Just wish I'd have planned ahead better and brought a change of clothes."

"Come on, let me buy you breakfast."

Ben thought of Jamie waiting for him in the room but didn't think revealing that to Steven was going to help anyone. Reluctantly Ben followed Steven into the dining room, searching his pockets for his cell phone so he could send Jamie a text. He swore to himself when he realized he must have left it in the room. With any luck, he'd finish here and get back to Jamie before she woke up.

Jamie woke with a smile on her face thinking of the warmth of Ben's arms. Her smile faded as she rolled over to an empty space where Ben had been hours ago. Jamie started to doubt herself. Was it only a dream? A very real fantasy? She felt silly but called out, "Ben?" The smell of sex still permeated the room, so she was sure it hadn't been her imagination.

When she received no answer, her face flushed with shame. He had left her again. She allowed herself no more than ten minutes self-pity, and then she got angry. She got out of bed and headed for the bathroom. She turned the shower to steaming hot and stepped in. As she soaped the washcloth and ran it over her body, she thought how his hands had touched her. She closed her eyes and could almost feel his fingers massaging her muscles, then turning tender, then probing.

Dammit! He wasn't even here but the thought of him aroused her. She washed the scent of him off her skin. She chastised herself for throwing herself at him again. She obviously hadn't learned her lesson after the first time. But at any rate, this time it was more satisfying… a lot more. He may have run away, but at least she'd had the best night's sleep in years. Just the thought of him inside of her made her grow wet. She turned the water colder and finished her shower.

Steven droned on about the success of the party. Ben resisted the urge to look at his watch again. He didn't want to be rude, or more importantly, give Steven any reason to suspect Ben hadn't spent the night alone. Ben was single so he wasn't worried about his reputation. He didn't know how Steven would respond to one of his star employees having an extramarital affair. Ben didn't want to cause Jamie any trouble.

As Steven ordered his third cup of coffee and began waxing about his latest brainstorm reference the direction of the company, Ben cut in. "Steven, can we continue this conversation on Monday? I'm anxious to get home and check on my sister."

Steven chuckled. "Always the big brother, aren't you? I understand. I'll walk with you. I was ready to leave anyway." Steven signaled for the check, and Ben groaned inwardly.

Chapter 32

The light was flashing on Jamie's answering machine when she walked in the door. Dropping her purse on the table, she pushed the button on her way to the refrigerator for water. Her mouth was dry from the amount of alcohol she had put away at the party.

Her stepfather's voice was shaky as he left a message. "Jamie, darling. I hate to leave this on your machine, but I don't have much time. Your mother has had a heart attack. She's at St. Joseph's Hospital in intensive care. She's holding on, but I think you should get here as soon as you can. I love you, honey." The click left Jamie in stunned silence.

She kicked herself into gear. Racing into her room she threw things into a suitcase and headed back out the door. She stopped long enough to let the neighbor know what happened and ask her to watch over the house while she was gone.

The drive was painfully long as she rushed to Richmond. She tried to reach her stepfather on his cell phone, but it went straight to voice mail. She realized he must be in the hospital where cell phones weren't allowed.

To fend off the dreaded thoughts of losing her mother, she pondered the mystery of Ben. She didn't think her heart could stand the touch-and-go relationship he must be used to. Didn't Susan warn her that he wasn't the settling down type? Could she be satisfied with casual sex? Extraordinary, fantastic sex? She might be able to if she didn't know Ben had so much more to offer.

She needed to talk this through with her mother. She always knew what to do. Then the tears came. Jamie thought of her mother, so energetic and full of love. She knew how to live life. She and her stepfather were regularly traveling. Her mother had always wanted to travel the world, and her stepfather supported her dream. When they were home, her mother volunteered for a variety of causes. She said it helped her remember to be thankful for what she had.

Jamie tried to be thankful. In spite of her failed marriage, she was thankful they didn't have kids who would suffer through the divorce. She was grateful no one else knew the humiliation she had experienced walking in on her husband wearing women's underwear with a dominatrix over him. She started laughing. With enough time and distance from the encounter, she could look back at the scenario and laugh at the ridiculousness of the situation. She might have to share it with her mother after all. Mom had never liked Eddie. She thought he was too "pretty." Mom was right. Jamie grinned.

Waiting as Steven drove off, Ben locked his car and rushed back into the hotel. The maid's cart parked in front of the room he and Jamie had shared the night before made his heart sink. He walked by and looked in. It was empty.

As he sped back to his house, he thought about how he was going to get ahold of Jamie. Her cell phone number was programmed in his cell phone, which she now had, and he didn't want to chance calling her at home and reaching her husband. The thought of waiting until Monday was torture. He could only imagine what she thought of him now.

Unlocking his apartment door, he went straight for his desk. He tore it apart in hopes of finding Jamie's business card but was disappointed. He sat in his chair and stared out the window, trying to think of his next move.

As Jamie got closer to the hospital, she gave in to the nagging desire to call Ben. She didn't want to appear needy, but she wanted to hear his voice. She wanted to listen to a plausible excuse of why he ran out on her that morning. The phone rang over and over before going to voice mail.

Back in the hotel room in D.C., the ringing phone vibrated the chair cushions.

Jamie left a short message, trying to sound matter-of-fact, with no hint of the hurt she was feeling. She let him know she'd be away for a few days but didn't ask anything of him. She didn't want him to feel pressured. She pulled into the hospital parking lot and said a short prayer before locking her car and going in.

The sterile smell of the hospital hit her as she floated through the electric doors. As she glanced around, the dazzling white of the walls contradicted the dark mood oozing from the patients and visitors in the waiting room. She stopped at the front desk and asked where to find her mother.

Jamie's stepfather, Bob, was in the sitting room reserved for the intensive care ward when Jamie stepped off the elevator. He wrapped his arms around her, and Jamie held him close. She pulled back and saw the dark circles under his eyes. He looked older than his sixty years.

"She's a fighter. She's still in a coma, but the doctors are hopeful. Thanks for coming. It means a lot to me and your mother."

She examined his wrinkled clothes and tussled hair. Giving his arm a squeeze, she said, "Why don't you go home and get some sleep? I'll stay with her. I promise I'll call if anything changes."

Bob gave her a tired smile. "I think I will. I at least need to change and take care of the cats. I'll be back soon. Call me if you hear anything new from the doctors." He gave her another quick hug and walked to the elevator.

Jamie watched him go, thankful her mother had found such a great guy. Bob treated her like a queen.

She turned to the nurses' desk to ask for an update on her mom. The nurse couldn't offer her any new information but escorted her into her mother's room. Jamie moved to the fake leather chair close to the bed that Bob had occupied for much of the night and day. There was a hospital-issued, white blanket crumpled in the seat. Jamie pushed it aside and sat down.

She took her mother's hand in her own and studied the lines. They were so familiar. These were the hands that held Jamie when she was scared. These hands smoothed her hair out of her face and wiped away the tears. Jamie leaned over and kissed the soft wrinkles that had just begun to show on her mother's cheek.

"Oh, Mom, I need to talk to you. You have to get better. I'm in a pickle only you would understand." Jamie looked into her mom's peaceful face. "There's this guy," she began with a sigh. "Guess you could have guessed that part."

Jamie rested her head on her mother's hand and tried to hold back the tears. She wasn't sure where to start. The nurse had told her that talking to her mother would be helpful. Research had shown brain waves are more active in comatose people when someone talks to them. That stimulation might be just what Betty needed to convince her brain to wake up.

She started hesitantly at first, with stops and starts. Even though she had visited her mom at Thanksgiving, she hadn't talked about Ben. They had kept their conversations light and focused on people Jamie had grown up with. Only a few times had they even discussed Eddie and Jamie's failed marriage. She was afraid to mention Ben because she didn't want her mom to think poorly of her. After all, she had met Ben while she was still married. Were her feelings for him considered cheating?

Finally, she couldn't hold it back anymore. She had held it all inside for so long, once she started talking about Ben, she couldn't stop. She poured out her heart, telling her mom about Ben's smile and how his eyes actually twinkled. When she got to the part about house shopping in Colorado, Jamie thought she felt her mom squeeze her hand. She stopped talking and studied the machines monitoring her mother. Seeing no other indications on the machines, she assumed she imagined it as part of wishful thinking.

She continued her story, skipping over the part about finding Eddie and his girlfriend. She wanted to save that story for when her mom could laugh along with her.

The nurse came in when Jamie was getting to the part about the Christmas party. Jamie patted her mom's hand. "I'll finish later." Jamie stood and stretched, surprised three hours had passed already. She decided to get a cup of coffee while the nurse was with her mom.

Monday morning couldn't come soon enough for Ben. He was in the office early but didn't see Jamie's car. He walked by her office a number of times trying to catch a glimpse of her to no avail. When he still hadn't spotted her by lunchtime, he went into her office suite.

Carolyn greeted him. "Mr. Simons, what can I do for you this afternoon?"

"I was wondering if Mrs. Woods had time for me?" he said self-consciously straightening his tie.

"I'm sorry. She's taken a few days off. I can make you an appointment for next week if you'd like."

"No, thank you. I'll send her an email."

Ben was concerned. Did Jamie feel so guilty about their night together that she couldn't even face him? Did her husband find out? He better not have done anything to Jamie. Ben felt himself getting angry at the thought. Jamie had never said Eddie was a violent man, but she didn't talk about him much at all. He wasn't sure what problems they had in their marriage but was convinced it had to be Eddie's fault. Jamie was everything he had ever wanted in a woman. He couldn't imagine any man not wanting her the same way.

When Bob returned close to midnight, he was clean-shaven and in fresh clothes. The bags under his eyes were a little lighter but still visible.

"Jamie, time for you to get some sleep. Go on over to the house," Bob said.

"Did you get any sleep?" Jamie asked.

"A little. But I'm able to doze here in the chair. I'm fine. Your timing was perfect. Why don't you go rest up and relieve me in the morning? Your room is ready at the house."

Jamie stood to hug him. "You are such a good man." He wrapped his arms around her and rubbed her back as if she were a little girl.

She leaned over to kiss her mother's forehead. She could smell the light scent of perfume her mother wore dabbed behind her ears. "I love you," she said, hoping her mom could hear her.

Jamie felt strange walking into her mom's empty house. Although she was an only child, her house was always the hub of activity. Neighbor kids were in and out, and Betty could be counted on to make up a special treat after school. Chocolate chip cookies were Jamie's favorites. Even after she went away to college, her mother would send her a care package with fresh cookies on a regular basis.

After the divorce, Betty didn't date, but she had lots of friends. She had ladies over for card club and she volunteered at the school and the church. She always seemed happy. It wasn't until she met Bob that Jamie felt her mom's attention somewhere other than on her. It was a tough time, but Jamie had to admit, high school was a tough time for any teenager.

To be fair, Jamie knew she was still her mother's top priority. She had faked sick a few times when her mom was looking forward to a date with Bob, so Betty had to call and cancel.

On the third incident, as Betty held Jamie in her arms before bedtime, Betty spoke to her in a storytelling rhythm. "I love you more than anything in the world and nothing will ever change that," came her soft-spoken voice. "I want you to grow up to be a strong, independent woman."

Jamie had snuggled closer into her mother's arms, proud of herself for winning her game.

"And because I love you so much, I won't let you turn into a spoiled brat."

Jamie was sure she had heard wrong. The inflection in Betty's voice didn't change as she continued. "Crying wolf is a dangerous thing. For the next few months, you're going to spend some afternoons volunteering as a candy-striper at the hospital in the children's ward. You'll see what it's like to really be sick."

With that, Betty gave her a huge squeeze and kissed the top of her head. "I love you. Sleep tight." She left Jamie speechless in her bed, only the nightlight from the bathroom breaking the darkness.

It was a very important lesson Jamie never forgot. After her months of forced servitude were over, she continued as a candy striper. She enjoyed making the kids laugh and bringing them cookies she had made.

Now she went into the kitchen and pulled a soda from the refrigerator. As she popped it open, she wandered aimlessly around the room. She inspected the door frame to the pantry. She could still make out the pencil marks on the wood commemorating her growth spurts. There were a few very close together. That was the time Jamie had insisted the superhero cereal she had convinced her mother to buy was making her grow at an increased speed. She smiled. Her mom was a good sport to go along with some of Jamie's crazy ideas, without ever spoiling the fun of it all.

She tossed the empty can in the recycle bin and shut off the lights. She picked up her bags where she had dropped them at the foot of the stairs when she entered and began the climb, remembering the creaks and groans from the floorboards.

The sadness threatened to overtake her again as she walked past her mother's room. Jamie touched the door, pushing it open. The bed was unmade, and the top blanket had slid to the floor. She went to work, making the bed and removing the water glass from the bedside table. She wanted things neat for when her mom came home from the hospital.

Chapter 33

Carolyn stopped Ben in the hall as he was entering the building the next morning, "Mr. Simons, did you ever get a hold of Mrs. Woods?"

"No, Carolyn, she hasn't answered my email. Is everything okay?"

"She called in a few minutes ago. She's fine, but her mother had a heart attack and is in a coma. She went to Richmond to be with her."

Ben's heart hurt with the news. He wanted to be with her, to comfort her. He knew she would be devastated.

Carolyn continued, "I'm sure this is hard on Mrs. Woods. She's very close to her mother."

Ben thanked her for the update and rushed to his office.

Jamie woke to the smell of coffee. She smiled and stretched. As her brain engaged, she remembered why she was here, and she threw her covers off. She slipped on her bathrobe as she went into the kitchen.

She stopped in her tracks. "What are you doing here?" she asked with undisguised disgust.

"Bob called my cell phone to ask where you were. He told me what happened, and I thought you might need someone to talk to. How's your mom?" Eddie asked.

Jamie was confused by this show of concern and took the cup of coffee handed to her without protest. She went back into the living room and stood staring into the empty fireplace.

Eddie came up behind her and stroked her shoulder.

She flinched as if burned. Spinning on her heels, her eyes drilled into him as she said, "Don't you ever touch me again!"

"Jamie, don't be like that. I want to be here for you."

"You weren't interested in being there for me when we were married. What's different now?"

Eddie was silent.

"Did your girlfriend kick you out?"

"She wasn't my girlfriend—"

Jamie held up her hand to stop him. "I don't want to hear it. It doesn't matter. You need to go. I have to get back to the hospital."

"Do you want me to go with you?"

Jamie looked at him in disbelief. "You do remember we're divorced, right? You have no right being here. You aren't part of this family anymore."

"Jamie, I'm sorry. I screwed up."

She shook her head. She couldn't believe this was happening. A year ago, she prayed for a chance to work things out with Eddie. She wanted to make it work, but he wouldn't give her the time of day. Now she was moving on and he wanted to fix things? This was too much.

She turned and stalked out of the room.

Eddie heard the door close and lock behind her. He walked around the living room examining the photos on the mantel and hanging on the wall above the couch. He had always loved the photo of Jamie with Betty at the beach. Jamie must have been fifteen or so. Her mom was trying to cover her bikini-clad body with a beach towel as Jamie fought her off. Someone had taken the picture while both women were smiling brightly. Off handedly, Eddie wondered who had taken the picture. He never thought to ask before.

He continued his tour down memory lane. This house was always warm and inviting. Thanksgiving was a very lonely place without having Jamie and her family to share it with. He didn't realize the little things would be what he missed the most.

His father was pretty upset when he found out Eddie and Jamie had split. The worst part was Eddie wasn't the one who told him. Jamie's father said something to him one day when they ran into each other at the clubhouse where they both still played golf.

There was hell to pay at Sunday dinner! His father thought the world of Jamie. Eddie couldn't very well tell him why she left. Thankfully, Jamie's dad must not have known the details or he would have shared them, and Eddie would surely have been cut off.

His father didn't come right out and say it, but there were a lot of threats about rewriting of wills and making other changes involving the family business. He did go so far as to insinuate Jamie's name wasn't the one that would get dropped.

He had to admit he missed having Jamie around to keep house for him and cook the meals. He hadn't given her enough credit for the things she did when they were married. Things he never thought of like picking up the dry cleaning or doing the laundry. That in itself wasn't enough to try to get her back for good, but the inheritance his father was holding over his head might be worth a few more years. His dad wasn't going to live forever. And Jamie wasn't bad, just boring.

Chapter 34

When Jamie returned to her mother's bedside, Bob's head rested on the bed, his hand covered Betty's. Jamie watched them both sleep for a while, thinking how blessed they were to have found each other.

Without picking up his head, Bob said, "We used to watch you sleep the same way."

"And I used to fake sleep, too," Jamie said.

"We knew."

He lifted his head and met her eyes. "She's getting stronger." He squeezed Betty's hand, then stood and stretched. "I need to make a few phone calls."

"Go. I'll be here as long as you need me. Mom and I have some catching up to do."

Bob patted Jamie's shoulder as he passed her. "I'll be back in a few hours. Call me if anything changes."

Jamie took his place in the chair. As the door closed, she told her mom, "You hit the jackpot with him, you know. He's a keeper."

Just after lunch, Ben approached the Reilly's house in Richmond. There were a lot of cars parked out front and he feared the worst. He hoped Jamie wouldn't be angry with him for coming and putting her in an uncomfortable spot with her husband, but he couldn't stay away, and she wasn't answering her cell. He'd been trying to reach her since Carolyn had told him about her mother.

Taking a deep breath, he got out of the car and slipped on his jacket. It was getting colder, and Ben could smell snow in the air. He was glad he had stopped at home to change out of his suit before starting the two-hour journey.

He approached the front door, not sure of the greeting he would receive. He waited patiently, trying to think of the right words to say.

The door was opened by a man in his early thirties, dressed in a pullover sweater and jeans. "Are you from the church?" he asked Ben.

The question threw Ben off, but he managed to reply, "No, I'm a friend of Jamie's. Is she here?"

Eddie eyed this newcomer suspiciously. "She's at the hospital with her mother." He offered his hand. "I'm Jamie's husband, Eddie. And you are?"

"Ben. Ben Simons. We work together." This was awkward. "How's Jamie's mom?"

"Getting better. Still not awake but all her vital signs are improving. You're welcome to come in and eat. Folks have been bringing food over all day."

"No thanks. I just wanted to see if Jamie needed anything. Looks like she has plenty of support."

"I've got it covered," Eddie said. "I'll tell her you stopped by."

Ben thanked him and turned to leave. He felt Eddie's eyes on the back of his neck the whole way to his car but refused to turn around. He put the car in drive and started his return trip, feeling foolish for trying to rush to Jamie's rescue when she obviously didn't need to be rescued.

Chapter 35

Jamie felt someone stroking her hair as her head lay next to her mother on the bed. She looked up expecting that Bob had returned. Surprised he wasn't there, she turned back to her mother's smiling face.

"Mom!" she cried. Jamie hugged her mother gently and kissed her face. "I've missed you."

"I'm not going anywhere without hearing about the Christmas party. How could you leave me hanging like that?" her mother joked. "Can I have some water?"

Jamie poured water into a cup and pushed the nurse's call button. As she held the straw to Betty's lips, the nurse came in. "Welcome back, Betty. Did you get enough sleep?"

"Plenty. Maybe next year we'll hire someone to decorate the house for Christmas. It wears me out."

Jamie slipped out of the room to call Bob while the nurse took Betty's vitals and made notes in her chart. When he answered, she heard voices in the background. She told him the good news, and he covered up the phone as he relayed the message to the house guests. A cheer went up and Jamie's heart was filled with happiness.

"I'll be right there," Bob said. "Tell Betty I'm bringing her something special from the Wilsons."

Jamie went back to her mother's room. The nurse completed her examination and hung the chart on a hook on the wall next to the bed. "The doctor will be along shortly." She smiled and slipped out the door.

Jamie took her mom's hand and sat gingerly on the bed. She couldn't stop smiling. "Bob's on his way, and he has something from the Wilsons."

Betty grinned. "Must be the apple tarts I adore. That means an extra few miles of walking this week," she said. "Now, tell me about this new fellow. Ben, is it? I'm afraid I didn't catch all the details. I was in and out. Maybe you should start from the beginning."

Jamie happily obliged. It was much more fun telling the stories when she could watch her mom's facial expressions and answer questions. Her mom made her think about things from a different perspective.

Bob arrived with three apple tarts in hand. He set them on the tray and leaned in to kiss Betty tenderly. "Don't ever do that again."

"I won't," she promised. "Nice to know you still appreciate me."

"More than you'll ever know," he whispered with tears welling in his eyes. He kissed her again and stood up straight, producing three forks from his jacket pocket. They all laughed and took a fork.

Jamie resumed her story telling, Bob also captured by the drama of it as he settled on the bed with his arm around his wife. This time she didn't skip the part about Eddie's affair. When she described the scene when she opened the bedroom door, Betty's eyes were wide, and she covered her mouth in surprise.

"You've got to be making this up," Bob said.

Jamie raised her right hand. "I swear it's the truth, the whole truth, and nothing but the truth. I can't get the picture out of my head." She made a gagging motion with the fork.

"Please tell me at least they weren't your panties?" her mom said.

"Gross! No!" Jamie hesitated. "At least I don't think so. Now I have to go back and throw out all my underwear, just in case!"

The three laughed and it felt wonderful.

The doctor came in and kicked Bob and Jamie out. Betty confessed she was getting tired, so they agreed to go home and visit her in the morning.

Bob and Jamie entered the quiet house expecting a mess from all the well-wishers who had stopped in that day. They were pleasantly surprised to find everything was neat and tidy, and the refrigerator was stocked with food. Bob made them both teas, and they took it in to the living room to relax.

"After everything you told us tonight about Eddie, I'm glad I kicked him out today."

"What?" Jamie blurted.

Bob looked up, afraid he said something wrong, but Jamie's anger wasn't directed at him.

"He was here when I woke up from my nap this afternoon. I told him I didn't think it was a good idea for him to be here, and I asked him to leave. He wasn't happy about it, but he left."

"He was here when I woke up this morning, and I told him to get out then. I'm sorry I didn't make sure he was gone when I left."

"Don't worry about it. I doubt he bears any ill-will toward us. But I'm not sure what he's up to. I heard him introduce himself to someone at the door as your husband."

Jamie rested her head on her hand. "What am I going to do with him?"

"Just keep saying no, honey. I don't think there is much else you can do," Bob said sympathetically. "But you might have some explaining to do at work. The guy at the door said he was a friend from the office. I didn't catch his name."

Jamie's stomach flipped. "Did you see him?"

"Briefly, through the front window. About your age. He was driving a blue RX-8." Bob studied the look on her face. "It was Ben, wasn't it?"

"I think so," she said hopefully.

"Go call him," Bob prodded. "Go."

Jamie got to her feet and kissed Bob's cheek. "Thank you for loving my mom," she said.

"I can't help it."

Jamie went to her room and closed the door. She pulled out her cell phone with shaking hands. She dialed Ben's number, but the phone went right to voice mail. She didn't bother leaving a message. What would she say? "I know you met my ex at my mom's house, but I didn't invite him." No, she needed to talk to him in person.

The next morning when Jamie got up, she found a note next to the coffee pot. "Went to the hospital. See you when you get up. Hope all went well with Ben."

Jamie rushed to get ready. She had slept longer than she intended but not very well. She had horrible dreams where she could see Ben, but he couldn't see or hear her.

Betty was sitting up in bed when Jamie arrived. Her hair had been washed, and she had on her own nightgown. She and Bob looked cozy. They sat holding hands as Bob read to her from a paperback. He put it down when she entered.

"Good morning," her mother said as Jamie leaned in to kiss her. "Bob told me about Eddie at the house. I'm sorry."

"Nothing for you to be sorry about. But Ben isn't answering his phone, so I don't know what he's thinking."

"Go to him, Jamie," her mother suggested. "I'm fine now. I'll be home soon. Maybe you can bring him down for Christmas."

Jamie's spirits lifted at the thought. "Are you sure?"

Betty laughed at the excitement in her daughter's face. "If it makes you this happy just to think about him, catch him and hold on."

Jamie hugged Betty and then Bob. "I love you both. I'll let you know how it works out!" She rushed out the door. She needed to gather her things before going back to Maryland.

Before she got on the road, she composed a short text to Ben.

"I have some explaining to do. Can we talk?" She hit send before she talked herself out of it.

On the drive home, Jamie's mind raced. How could she explain all this to Ben? Had they even talked about the divorce yet? Things happened so quickly the night of the party, and it certainly wasn't the right time to talk about Eddie. Now Ben must think the worst of her—a married woman willing to have a fling after a night of drinking. She was going to have to convince him it wasn't a fling, and she definitely wasn't married anymore.

Chapter 36

Eddie sat in his car with the engine running. It was cold and getting colder as the sun went down. "Doesn't this guy have a life?" he muttered. "How late does he work?"

The parking lot was nearly empty outside the Winkler and Stein building. Eddie had never been inside but had dropped Jamie off once in a while so knew where the employees' entrance was behind the building. Her spot was empty so she must still be in Richmond.

As he tried to warm his hands in front of the heater vents, he stewed about this Ben guy. It had to be his fault that their marriage fell apart. Jamie would never be brave enough to make a decision like that on her own. He wondered how long they had been screwing each other.

The back door opened and the figure he had been waiting for appeared. He was carrying a laptop bag in one hand and swinging his keys in the other.

Eddie opened his car door and walked on a path to intercept Ben.

The cell phone vibrated in Ben's pocket as he pushed open the back door to the office building. He pulled it out, surprised to receive a text from Jamie.

He tapped out a reply.

Looking up, Ben noticed the figure approaching him. There was something familiar about him, but no real recognition set in. It wasn't until the man stepped into the circle of illumination made by the parking lot lights that Ben got a good look at him. The sight of Eddie stopped him in his tracks.

His first thought was something bad must have happened to Jamie. Why else would her husband be here at this time of night? "What's happened? Is Jamie all right?" Ben asked.

"Why the hell would I tell you anything?" Eddie snapped and kept approaching.

Ben was confused. Then a thought dawned on him. *Shit, he knows about the Christmas party.*

"If you've done anything to Jamie—" he started.

"Don't threaten me, you son of a bitch! Things were going fine until you came along."

This was Ben's worst nightmare. He never meant to cause Jamie any pain or to mess with her marriage. But now there was no going back. "Seems to me if things were fine, you wouldn't be skulking around in the dark."

Eddie's fist landed squarely on Ben's jaw, whipping his head around and knocking him back several steps.

The blow caught Ben off guard, and he dropped his computer and keys in the snow as he tried to catch his balance. Before he was able to regain fully, Eddie was on him again, this time landing a punch in the gut.

"Come on, you sissy. What are you waiting for?"

Ben stood and blocked Eddie's next swing with his left forearm, stepping in with a right uppercut to Eddie's abdomen. A rush of air escaped his lips. Ben stepped back. "Listen, I didn't mean for this to happen." Ben tried to deescalate the situation.

Eddie looked up at him from his doubled over position, catching his breath. Then he attacked, trying to catch Ben off guard again. Ben was ready for it this time and landed a punch into Eddie's face. He heard something crack.

"You bastard!" Eddie screamed clutching at his nose. Blood oozed from between his fingers. Eddie shook out his hands and blood left red spots in the dirty white snow. His glare burned a hole into Ben. "You had no right to get between us."

"You're right, I didn't," Ben admitted. "I didn't mean to. But Jamie deserves so much more than you're giving her. Can't you see what a treasure you have?"

Eddie spit blood into the snow. "Treasure?" he said with disgust. "She was hardly a treasure. Always wanting to go places together, needing attention, bugging me about kids. The only thing she was good for was to keep the housework up and cook my meals."

Ben was disgusted. He couldn't believe Jamie would have fallen for a guy like this, let alone stay with him. What was she thinking?

His anger overtook him, and he landed a quick jab into Eddie's gut. The give of his soft belly gave Ben a sense of satisfaction.

It didn't last long as Eddie stood swinging. His left fist made contact with Ben's ribs, but Ben was able to turn away to avoid the right.

Eddie yelled in frustration, "You're a piece of shit with nothing. What did you do to convince her to leave me?"

Confusion swept over him. Leave him? What was he talking about?

"The little bitch wasn't free for more than a month when you started snooping around."

Free? What was he saying? Jamie had left Eddie?

Eddie saw the dazed expression on Ben's face and took advantage of it. Ben reacted late and took the full brunt of the punch in the jaw, knocking him off his feet. As he landed in the crusty snow, his head hit the case of his laptop.

Eddie kicked him in the ribs. "You can have her," he spat.

Ben watched him storm off as darkness overcame him. His last thought was that he now had a chance to make Jamie happy.

Chapter 37

"Ben, what happened to your face?" Trina asked with concern, reaching her hand to touch the bruise on his jawline.

"A slight disagreement."

"I hope you won."

Ben smiled. "I think I have."

Trina gave him a questioning look but didn't push it. "Want to get out of the office for a while?" she asked.

He looked at her out of the corner of his eye.

"I need a favor. My brother is moving to town, and he asked me to go check out a house for him. I'm horrible at that sort of thing. I can tell you if it looks nice, but I don't know the first thing about checking the plumbing and the roof. The realtor said she'd meet me at four-thirty today but she's showing it again at seven, and I don't want to mess this up."

Ben glanced at his watch. He didn't feel like being at work. It was a good excuse to leave a few minutes early and give him a chance to think about Jamie.

"Where is it? I'll follow you over."

Trina handed him a slip of paper. "I'll meet you there. I have to run another errand first. The realtor said the door will be open." She squeezed his arm in a gesture of thanks and moved off down the hall, very pleased with herself.

Ben drove through the peaceful neighborhood looking for the address. The houses were well-kept and yards neatly manicured. He saw signs of kids, but they must have been tucked inside away from the lightly falling snow. The trees lining the streets were probably gorgeous in the fall when the leaves changed colors. Now they were barren but outlined in snow.

He found the address and turned into the driveway. There were tire tracks leading up to the closed garage door. The realtor must be taking advantage of the empty garage. Ben parked and went up the front walk. It was lined with waist high hedges neatly clipped. He rang the doorbell and waited but no one answered. He tried the door handle. It was unlocked as promised.

"Hello?" he called as he stepped in and closed the door behind him. There was a light on in the next room and Ben headed toward it, slipping off his overcoat. He heard a click behind him and turned as a hand rotated the deadbolt.

The room was dark but there was a distinctively female figure silhouetted by the porch light coming through the glass of the door.

"Trina, I'm not in the mood for games."

"What if it isn't a game?" the voice asked huskily as she approached.

Ben felt a stirring that was an automatic response now to the sound of her voice. Jamie stepped out of the shadows and stood within inches of Ben.

She put her hands on his chest and took in the marks on his face. "What happened?"

Ben placed his finger on her lips. "Shhh, it doesn't matter. What did you want to talk about?"

She stared into his eyes as her fingers worked the buttons of his shirt.

He dropped his jacket and his hands ran up her bare arms to the tiny silk straps on her shoulders. His mind reeled as he tried to take it all in. She had finished with the buttons and was now running her fingers through the hair on his chest. His hands followed the straps to the material covering her chest. He must be dreaming. His fingers brushed her nipples and they hardened. He slid his hands under her breasts and let his thumbs play over the points.

She slid her hands down and was working at the belt and then his zipper. The bulge in his pants wasn't making it any easier for her to maneuver. A small moan escaped his lips as his desire grew. He took her face in his hands and kissed her, gently at first but then with passion as the surge overtook him. She kissed him back just as deeply, walking him backwards until he felt a wall behind him.

When he couldn't go any further, her hands made their way to his hips and she pushed his pants and boxers free in one motion. Ben never stopped kissing her as his hands explored her body and the little material covering it. He wanted to slow down and enjoy the sight, but he also didn't want to let her get away.

She tilted her head back, and Ben attacked her neck with nibbles and kisses. Her hands were quivering as they reached between his legs to grasp him firmly. He gasped and was attentive as she stroked him, tenderly at first but then with more purpose as his liquid gave her lubrication.

His fingers explored the wetness between her legs, and he longed to be surrounded by her. He spun her around so her back was to the wall. As he pushed his body close to hers, he managed to kick off his shoes.

Jamie's hands wrapped around his neck, and she continued to kiss him. He placed one hand on the back of her thigh and lifted her leg to rest over his hip. In one swift motion, he lifted her other leg, supporting her weight with his legs, her back braced against the wall.

His hands slid under her buttocks and guided her downward. Jamie was trembling with expectation as she felt his tip enter her. Her hips rocked, and she felt a mix of relief and satisfaction as he plunged into her. She was lost in the feeling of him, the touch of him, and the promise of what was yet to come.

In no time, Jamie felt the hot rush building in her, but she could sense Ben was holding back. At that moment, she couldn't focus on his needs. Her whole body was yearning for release. Ben moved in and out of her with such precision, as if he were reading her desires.

Jamie gave in and let herself go as Ben held her close. She cried out his name as she exploded in orgasm. He didn't release her until the final spasms of her delight subsided. Slowly he lowered her feet to the ground.

"You're holding back on me," Jamie whispered, feeling his erection still pressing into her.

"I didn't exactly plan for this when I came to look at a house."

"I did," she breathed. "We're safe." Jamie had been on birth control for years now, and it had never failed her. "Besides, a little late to think about that now, isn't it?"

She slipped away from him, and he felt her slide down his body, the silk of her lingerie teasing him further. Before he could protest, she took him into her mouth, her tongue caressing the underside of his shaft.

His fingers clasped her head as he tried to slow down her movements, so it didn't end too soon. He wanted to be inside of her—really inside.

She was determined, and he couldn't hold out any longer. She felt him release and tasted the saltiness of him. She drank deeply and didn't let go until his legs were shaking. She pulled back, her tongue never stopping.

When he couldn't take it anymore, he pulled her to her feet and kissed her. When they came up for breath, he managed to say, "I'm glad to see you too."

She smiled at him. "Do you want to explore the rest of the house?"

"There's more?"

Jamie smiled at him coyly. "Much more," she whispered, letting her tongue flicker over his ear.

"Dammit," he breathed. "I don't think my legs can take much more."

"You can rest in here," Jamie said as she led the way into what must have been the master bedroom. Like the rest of the house, it was devoid of furniture, but the built-in bookcases and fireplace separating the room from the bathroom gave it a romantic feel.

In the center of the room, a tablecloth was adorned by a plate of strawberries and a fondue pot of chocolate. Ben smiled wolfishly. "Is this to keep up my strength?"

"You'll need your nourishment," Jamie assured him.

Ben sat on the floor and reached for a strawberry. He dipped it in the chocolate and bit it off at the stem. "Almost perfect," he said.

"Almost?"

"We need to talk." He wouldn't meet her eyes. He picked up another strawberry and studied it.

She waited while he determined the best way to broach the subject. "I met your husband." He didn't look at her.

"He's my ex-husband," Jamie corrected him.

Ben's eyes met hers. "He said he was your husband."

"Maybe he's having doubts, but I'm not. The divorce was final more than a month ago."

"Why was he—"

Jamie cut him off. "Who knows why he does what he does. I told him to leave. There's no place for him in my life anymore."

"You should have told me," he said.

"I wanted to. I tried, but I thought you were with someone else. I didn't think you were interested."

He laughed in disbelief. "How many more ways could I have shown you I was interested? That I wanted you."

"You left me the morning after the Christmas party," Jamie whispered.

He shook his head vigorously. "I didn't leave you. Steven bagged me when I went to get you breakfast. By the time I got away from him, you were gone."

He reached out his hand, and Jamie took it.

"My phone was gone too so I thought you had it. I couldn't figure out how to reach you without calling your house and chancing your husband would answer."

"Ex," she corrected him.

"Well, I didn't know, did I? It slipped your mind to share that detail with me."

"I wasn't thinking about Eddie that night."

"Damn good thing." He pulled her into his lap. With his other hand he dipped another strawberry and held it out for Jamie. She looked into his eyes as she first licked the chocolate suggestively before sucking the strawberry into her mouth very slowly.

"Dammit!" Ben said, rolling her over and covering her body with his. He was recovering already.

She finished her strawberry and kissed him fully, allowing him to enjoy the strawberry taste from her mouth. Then she pushed on his chest. "You'll never see the whole house at this rate."

"I don't need anything else." He buried his face into her neck.

"It'll be worth it."

He rolled off and she got agilely to her feet. She slipped one strap off her shoulder and then the other. She allowed the silk to glide down her body, letting it fall to her feet and stood before him naked. She stepped back as Ben reached out to touch her.

Then she turned and was gone. Ben heard the shower start. He couldn't believe this was happening. After a few short minutes, he stripped off his shirt and made his way into the master bath. The room was large with a Jacuzzi tub surrounded by bay windows opening into an enclosed backyard. Ben assumed no one could see in but didn't spend much time pondering the question. He looked through the steamy glass of the shower at Jamie's stunning body beaded in water as she watched him. He took his time, enjoying the sight until Jamie turned away self-consciously. Only then did he open the shower door and join her, slipping his arms around her soapy waist.

The feel of her slippery and wet in his grasp brought him to full attention in no time. He licked the droplets from her neck, causing her to squirm. Her hands roamed freely across his chest and down his stomach. When her lathered hands grasped his manhood, he inhaled sharply. She slid her hands expertly up and down his shaft. He stopped kissing her as his attention was concentrated on her movements. Just when he didn't think he could take it any longer, she suddenly released him. He opened his eyes to her mischievous grin.

"After you've dried off, I have more to show you." She slipped out of the shower before Ben had a chance to react. He took a few deep breaths to get himself under control.

Jamie wrapped herself in a towel and disappeared out the door.

He watched after her, wondering what she was up to next. He rinsed and shut off the water. He toweled off and went in search of her, not bothering to cover up.

He walked through the dining room, following sounds into the kitchen. Jamie was sitting on the kitchen counter, her towel slipping in a very seductive manner, sipping a glass of champagne. "Want some?" She held a glass out to him.

"Definitely," he growled. He took advantage of her hands being occupied to loosen the towel, unwrapping her like the gift she was. He buried his face in her cleavage, appreciating the smell of her.

Jamie giggled and struggled to set the glasses down without spilling the drinks. By the time she had navigated that, Ben had worked his way down to her stomach and was lavishing her with kisses. "Like the granite countertops?" she asked.

"Very much," he responded without stopping his route. He spread her legs. Jamie was wet with anticipation. His tongue warmed her senses and sent a shock of electricity through her body. She grasped his head between her hands and tangled her fingers in his hair. It took no urging for Ben to bury his face deeper and let his tongue split her lips to find the liquid inside.

She gasped and thrust her hips upward. Ben had a firm hold on her hips to control the timing. He wanted to torture her the same way she had been torturing him...and enjoy every minute of it.

When he felt she had suffered enough, Ben repositioned one of his hands to slip a finger inside her. Her intake of breath told him it was almost time. He slipped another finger in and moved them in and out while continuing his attention with his tongue. As she exploded into him, his tongue worked overtime to keep up with her juices. As her orgasm ended, she tried to push him away from her over sensitive nerve endings. He wasn't quite finished and continued long, slow traces with his tongue, sending shivers through her body.

Worn out, Jamie pulled Ben's face up to hers and kissed him. Ben pushed himself against her and felt the heat between her legs. He was rock hard again and wanted to feel her from the inside. He pulled her hips to the end of the counter. She laid back on the cold granite and let him position her legs over his shoulders. He watched her face as he entered her.

Jamie tried to pull him closer, but her legs were still weak and shaking from her climax. Instead she relaxed and allowed him to get into a rhythm to suit his needs. His pumping became more intense until he suddenly became still. His eyes were closed and his breathing heavy.

A laugh escaped her lips as she watched him try to get control of himself. She let her feet drop and pulled away from him. She slipped off the counter and kissed him again.

With a playful look, she said, "You haven't even seen the view of the backyard." She turned her back on him and stared out the window over the sink. Ben couldn't resist the sight of her. He slipped his arms around her from behind, and she felt him hard against her. She leaned forward, allowing him easier access. His hands slid to her hips as she reached between her legs to guide him in. The gentle rhythm began. By now Jamie had recovered enough to begin the buildup of sexual expectancy again.

She leaned over the counter more and held onto the sink with both hands as she rocked with him. He slid one hand around front and teased her until they climaxed together. Afterwards, he turned her to face him so he could hold her in his arms. They clung to each other, breathless and worn out. "You're going to be the death of me at this rate," he said wearily.

They heard a car pull into the drive. Jamie and Ben exchanged looks. "Another surprise?" Ben asked with a quirky grin.

Jamie put her hands in the center of Ben's chest and gave him a shove. "The realtor!"

In a flurry they dashed to the bedroom and grabbed their clothes. They heard the door handle jiggle, then the sound of someone rummaging for keys.

"Jamie?" they heard the realtor call. "Jamie? Are you here?"

"In the kitchen."

When the realtor entered the kitchen, Jamie and Ben were leaning against the kitchen island—this time with most of their clothes.

"Well? What do you think? It's a nice neighborhood."

"We'll take it," Ben said.

Both women's heads snapped up to look at Ben.

"What?" Jamie asked in disbelief.

"We'll take it. When can we move in?"

Ben kept his gaze focused on the realtor. He could feel Jamie's eyes searching his face.

"Ben, shouldn't we—" He took her hand and squeezed it.

The second woman recovered quicker than Jamie. "Well, as you can see, the owners have already moved out so it's just a matter of getting the required loan paperwork completed. The inspections have been accomplished. You have the right to have your own done if you prefer." She pulled out a stack of papers from her briefcase. "In order to hold the house, I need you to make an official offer in writing." She handed the paperwork to Ben.

He took a few minutes to read it over while Jamie looked over his shoulder. Then he scribbled a figure on the offer line and signed the document. As he handed it back, he said, "Why don't we come by the office on Monday and start the paperwork?"

The owner took the documents and placed them in her briefcase. "Sounds like a plan." She set a business card on the counter and extended her hand.

As Ben shook it, he asked, "Do you mind if we stay a while longer and look around some more?"

"Of course not. It'll be yours soon enough anyway. Just lock the key in the lock box on your way out." With that, she gathered her things and left, before they could change their minds.

Ben turned to stare into Jamie's eyes. He had acted impulsively but it felt so right. He didn't want to let another day go by without Jamie.

She shook her head. "You're crazy, Ben Simons."

"Yes I am. Think you can live with that?"

"It'll be fun to try."

He kissed her. When they came up for breath, she asked, "Do you want to see the rest of the house?"

Ben smiled. "So many rooms, so little time."

############

About the Author

Dawn Brotherton is an award-winning author and featured speaker at writing and publishing seminars. When it comes to exceptional writing, Dawn draws on her experience as a retired colonel in the US Air Force as well as a softball coach. Her books include the Jackie Austin Mysteries, *The Road to Publishing*, and the *Softball Scoresheet.* She is a contributing author to the non-fiction *A-10s over Kosovo*, sharing stories from her deployment. She has also written the middle grade Lady Tigers Series about girls' fastpitch softball, encouraging female athletes to reach for the stars in the game they love. For more information about Dawn's books and book signings, check out her website www.DawnBrothertonAuthor.com.

www.ingramcontent.com/pod-product-compliance
Lightning Source LLC
Chambersburg PA
CBHW071148180726
48291CB00007B/2368

9781939696533